march 2010

D0966840

DISCARDED

APRIL'S HOPE

HOME TO HEATHER CREEK

APRIL'S HOPE

Robert Elmer

Guideposts

NEW YORK, NEW YORK

Acknowledgments

My mother—who was born on an island in Denmark, in the month of April—has always reminded me through her life's example that "Love bears all things, believes all things, hopes all things, endures all things" (1 Corinthians 13:7, ESV). Even before I learned the words to that verse, she lived them for everyone to see. To me she is, and will always be, April's Hope.

—Robert Elmer

Home to Heather Creek

APRIL'S HOPE

Chapter
One

D on't touch that, Grandma!"
Christopher scooted his chair away from the
breakfast table and nearly fell over as he pointed at
the sink. "Isn't it Emily's turn to do the dishes?"

Charlotte Stevenson paused for a moment, her cast-iron
frying pan in hand. She wondered why the morning's
chores suddenly seemed so important to her younger
grandson. Would that he had cared this much about cleaning the barn yesterday or about caring for Toby and
Lightning.

"I don't think so, dear." She lowered the frying pan into
the scarred porcelain sink, where it would most likely
require a good soak to dislodge the remains of a half-dozen
eggs. Her three grandchildren could really put away the
eggs.

"And even if it was," she added, "you kids are already
going to be late for school. Don't worry. I'll do them today."

Best they take me up on it, she thought, knowing she didn't
often make this kind of offer, especially now that her
grandchildren had been living with them at Heather Creek

Farm for . . . Goodness, had it already been a year since Denise's funeral had brought these three to their door?

Apparently her offer wasn't good enough for Christopher though. Suddenly his seventeen-year-old brother, Sam, stood up from the table as well, the same kind of panicked urgency written all over his face.

What in the world . . . ? Charlotte wondered.

"Really, Grandma," Sam told her in no uncertain terms. He tried to wave her away from the sink, just as Christopher had done. "Emily can take care of it today."

"Yeah," echoed Christopher. "Emily can do it."

Fourteen-year-old Emily was looking from her older brother to her younger brother in obvious confusion.

Charlotte had already piled most of their breakfast dishes in the sink and was ready to shoo the kids out of the kitchen. On a busy morning like this, she could use a little peace—and didn't mind plunging her arms into some hot suds to find it.

"No!" Christopher lunged for her just as she moved the frying pan under the faucet and turned on the water. But he was too late to stop the brisk spray of cold water that hit his grandmother squarely in the stomach. As it soaked through her yellow terry robe she tumbled backward in shock before catching her balance on the table behind her. Still the cascade soaked her as if she had just stepped in front of a showerhead.

"Turn it off, Christopher!" Sam ordered his little brother. Meanwhile, Emily screeched and scrambled for cover while Christopher skittered around the edge of the spray.

"I'm trying!" Christopher yelled back. But by then the

unexpected shower had created a sizable puddle on the faded yellow-and-white linoleum. Christopher lunged toward the sink, and slipped on the water. In a windmill of panic he reached out to grab his grandmother, but between the two of them Charlotte could hardly keep her own footing, much less Christopher's.

Just then, Charlotte's grown son, Pete, stepped in through the back door. He paused in the doorway, his lanky frame silhouetted by the dim April morning, and took it all in with a curious expression.

"What are you guys doing in here?" he asked, rubbing a hand over a two-day beard, as if he encountered this kind of thing every day. "Taking a shower?"

Charlotte ignored his question; by this time she had managed to creep up on the sink from the side. She turned off the water with a deft flick of her wrist. She still had no clue what had just happened, but now they all were soaked.

Sam and Christopher looked as if they had just stepped in from taking a walk in the pouring rain without benefit of raincoats or umbrellas. Emily seemed to have avoided the worst of it, an honor that had fallen to a dripping-wet Charlotte. She picked up the nearest dishtowel to dry her face and her short, graying hair but quickly realized that the towel was soaking wet too.

Pete just stood in the doorway, letting in the chilly air and looking from one wet person to the next. And then he began to laugh.

"Pete!" Charlotte reprimanded her son. "The least you could do is grab something to help us mop up this mess."

But Pete had doubled over in laughter, saying something about the "oldest gag in the book" as he stepped through the water to get to the sink. He pulled up the sink's spray wand from its slot to the right of the faucet.

"Check this out." He unraveled a short ribbon of black electrical tape, nearly invisible where it had been wrapped around the black lever. "This held the lever in the 'on' position, so when you turned on the water . . ." He demonstrated with a shot of water into the sink.

Sam and Christopher were edging slowly toward the far door. Only their uncle's raised hand stopped them from quietly disappearing.

"I always wanted to do something like this for April Fools' Day," Pete went on, holding up the tape for all to see. "I just never had the nerve when I was a kid. My mom would have killed me."

"Pete," said Charlotte, "that's a little extreme, don't you think? I would never have dreamed of such a thing, even if you did deserve it more than once."

Pete just shrugged as Emily held up her own hands and shook her head, innocence written all over her face.

"Don't look at me," she told them. "I had no idea what was going on here until just now."

All eyes turned to the boys.

"You weren't supposed to do that, Grandma," Sam suddenly blurted out. "It was supposed to be a joke on her. On Emily."

He motioned to his sister and went on.

"If Emily would have just done the dishes the way she was supposed to, none of this would have happened."

He shrugged. "Well, maybe it would have happened, just not to you."

"So I was the one who was supposed to get all wet?" said Emily, crossing her arms. "And I suppose you think that's funny."

"He thought of it." Christopher did his best to deflect the blame.

Pete pushed a towel around on the floor with the toe of his boot. "I don't know if that sounded like an apology or not, Mom." The hint of a smile curled at the corners of Pete's mouth again as he mopped the floor in his own sort of way. "But for a minute there, you all looked pretty funny."

No one said anything until Christopher whispered, "April Fools'?"

Pete began to laugh again, and the kids followed his lead when Charlotte eventually managed a smile. Well, maybe she could see a little humor in it. Soon they had her laughing, loud and long.

"It was on this Web site," explained Christopher, gasping for breath between giggles. "A hundred best April Fools' jokes. We picked the one that didn't have gross stuff in it, like shaving cream or frogs, but there was this other one that . . ."

"Okay, okay, that's enough." Charlotte checked her watch and herded the kids out of the kitchen. "You have exactly three minutes to brush your teeth and get going to school. And you'd better watch yourselves when you get back home. I used to know a few good April Fools' Day pranks myself."

The veiled threat stopped Christopher in his tracks, and he stared up at his grandmother with wide eyes.

"No way. Did they have April Fools' Day when you were little?"

She gave him a gentle push out the door, doing her best to keep a straight face.

"As a matter of fact, they did. And I'm just giving you fair warning. When you're least expecting it, you boys just might find yourselves on the receiving end, if you're not careful."

"You wouldn't."

Christopher looked back at her as if she couldn't possibly be serious, but she didn't give him a chance to find out.

"Go now," she told the kids with a sweeping motion. "And Sam, you drive carefully. We've seen enough fooling from you for one day."

Threats duly delivered, Charlotte turned back to see Pete twiddling the dial of the old ivory tabletop Philco radio they kept in the kitchen, more for show than anything else. Its amber dial glowed in a way that often warmed up an ordinary radio broadcast. Charlotte had no idea how old the thing was; it had belonged to Bob's father at some point. Then, as now, it was good for listening to the daily grain reports, though Pete knew as well as anyone that the 6:00 AM show had ended at least an hour ago.

Pete looked up at her with a question in his eyes. "You surprise me sometimes, Mom. All this mess and you just let them go."

"What else can I do?" She asked the obvious. "They have to get to school."

"Hmm. Well, I'm not sure I believe what you told the boys. You never told me you did any April Fools' jokes when you were young."

"Didn't I?" She returned to her dishes, this time making sure the tape had been completely removed from the spray grip. Truth was, she thought she might have played an innocent joke or two on her older brother Chet when they were ten or twelve. Chet was always doing that sort of thing, and he reminded her a little of Pete, come to think of it. But they had done nothing more serious than putting salt in the sugar bowl. Pete adjusted the dial on the ancient radio until he apparently located the news station he wanted.

"Looking for anything in particular?" she asked.

He held up his hand and leaned closer to the speaker. "Weather report," he whispered as a serious-sounding male reporter cut in with details about frontal systems approaching from northern Nebraska and areas of weakening low pressure across the state. "I heard there's some serious rain on the way."

"Oh?" She looked out the kitchen window at the fallow fields in front of Heather Creek Farm, squinted at the friendly morning sun, and wondered if the forecast could be mistaken. "A few April showers might be nice."

"No, Mom." When he shook his head, his unusually serious expression made her pause. "I don't think we're talking just some April showers. From what I hear, we're going to get more rain out there than you just got in here. Serious stuff. Our fields could get totally washed out if we try to plant too soon."

That could be devastating, but she also knew they couldn't wait much longer to plant their annual corn crop. Pete's tone brought her up short, and she said no more. Obviously this was no April Fools' prank.

Chapter Two

By midafternoon, Charlotte had almost decided the weather forecasters had been mistaken. She still couldn't see any storm clouds, only blue skies accented by high, wispy cirrus tails every time she checked out the kitchen window.

"Who needs April showers, eh, Lightning?" While Christopher's brown tabby rubbed against her leg, Charlotte pulled a sheet of newly baked sugarless oatmeal-raisin cookies from the oven, yelped at the heat that scorched through her hot pad, and dropped them unceremoniously to the cutting board.

"Well, Bob had better appreciate them," she said to herself as she carefully scooped each cookie to a paper towel on the counter. Amazing how a little blended cinnamon, spices, oatmeal and raisins could turn out. She also added unsweetened applesauce, and plenty of it, to make up for the sugar her diabetic husband couldn't eat.

Resisting the temptation to pop yet another one into her mouth, she had piled a few of the already cooled cookies onto a small plate and was headed for the back door when the phone rang.

"Would you please get that for me?" She paused and looked down at the expectant cat, who only meowed to be let out.

Well, if Lightning couldn't make herself useful ... Charlotte stepped over the cat's tail, set the cookies down on the counter, and snapped up the phone on the fourth ring.

"I'm sorry," the woman on the other end of the line announced after Charlotte said hello. "Sounds as if I caught you in the middle of something."

"Not at all," Charlotte wasn't aware she sounded quite that breathless, but the stranger went on to introduce herself as Julie Gauge, the general manager of the Farm Family Foundation. Had Charlotte heard of the organization? she asked.

"I ... think so, but ..." She hesitated, wondering what kind of donation she would be asked for and whether she should ask to be put on a do-not-call list. Weren't telemarketers supposed to abide by such a list?

"Actually," the woman went on as if reading Charlotte's mind, "I'm not calling about a donation, if that's what you're thinking." She laughed pleasantly, which put Charlotte a little more at ease. *What then?*

"I'm calling to tell you that you and Mr. Stevenson have been chosen as the Adams County Farm Family of the Year."

Well, Charlotte certainly knew what *that* meant, although it had been several years since she and Bob had been to one of those lovely Farm Family of the Year open houses. Something had always come up, it seemed.

"Mrs. Stevenson? Are you still there?"

"Yes, of course." Charlotte brought her mind back to the phone call. "That sounds wonderful. This means—"

"—that you will be receiving a year's supply of FarmFresh butter, a fifty-dollar gift certificate from Home Depot, a twenty-five-dollar gift certificate from Central Nebraska Veterinary Services . . ."

"Thank you so much, Miss Gauge." Charlotte tried to sound polite. "We never win anything."

"Please! If you call me Julie, I'll call you Charlotte."

"Of course, uh, Julie."

"But of course this means you'll be hosting the upcoming open house at your farm. That's actually why I'm calling." Now it was Julie's turn to hesitate. "Truth is, we had a cancellation from the family we had initially lined up for the event. They just called us this morning to tell me they couldn't do it, after all. Some . . . family issues, I think."

Oh. So the Stevensons were apparently Plan B.

"We'll do everything we can to help you with the planning, of course." Julie Gauge took a deep breath and went on. "I'll be coordinating the different community groups who will join in, the FFA, the school groups . . ."

"School groups?" Charlotte asked. "I thought the open house was normally in the middle of summer."

"Normally, yes. This year, however, the executive board decided we needed to include school groups, bring them out to the farm. You know, show the kids what our agricultural heritage is all about. Sort of an all-American field trip."

"I see."

"We both know that a lot of kids in towns and urban settings really have no idea what goes on at a working farm, even though they live just a few miles away. Even here in

Nebraska, if you can believe that. They might know what it smells like, if the wind is blowing the wrong direction, but as far as the day-to-day operation . . ."

Her voice trailed off, prompting Charlotte to speak up. "I know what you mean. Our own grandchildren from California have learned so much in the past year."

"Exactly!" Julie's voice went up an octave. "See, that's exactly why I'm so excited that you and Robert will be the farm family this year. You're both so down-to-earth, and you know what it's like to reach out to people who don't know farming. That's exactly what we need. So . . . I'll put you down as a yes?"

Charlotte was about to open her mouth when a thought occurred to her.

"Wait a minute." She dimpled a still-warm cookie with her finger. "If school groups are coming, that means you want it to happen before June, correct?"

Charlotte thought she heard the other woman gulp before answering.

"As I mentioned, the schedule this year is slightly mod-ified compared to last year, yes. But the good news is that you won't have to worry about any of the publicity, since that's all done. In fact, the flyers are all printed. All we have to do is print up a little sticker to change the name and address of the host farm. Now, Stevenson is spelled with a *v* rather than a *p-h*, is that correct? I want to make sure all the flyers are done right."

"Yes, but . . . how soon would it be? The kids get out of school the first week of June, I believe. Just before that?"

Another pause, as Julie seemed to fudge her words.

"You could say that. Just before school lets out."

"How much before school lets out?" Charlotte didn't want to sound rude, but what was the big mystery, after all?

"Saturday the twenty-fifth," Julie finally blurted out. "Three weeks from now."

"I'm sorry, I don't think I understood you correctly. You didn't mean that the open house is actually scheduled for three weeks from *now*, did you?"

Again Julie hesitated. "Actually, yes. But as I said, you wouldn't have a thing to worry about. Typically the FFA kids are willing to come and help with crowd control. That's the way it works at open houses all over the state. I'm sure you'll be able to recruit several women's groups to help sell food, and I know the Extension people will be happy to do one of their plant-identification demonstrations."

She of course meant the volunteers from the Adams County branch of the University of Nebraska Cooperative Extension, who knew a bit of everything about growing seasons, seed types, fertilizers, plant diseases, and just about anything else you could think of.

Julie went on: "Perhaps some of the ladies from the Heather Creek Grange will join in with one of their quilt displays, or we could invite the Scouts, and a couple of church groups, or—"

"Oh dear." Now Charlotte understood what the woman had been hemming and hawing about. *Only three weeks?* "We'd have so much planning to get all those groups to show up on such short notice. And we still have a lot of cleanup to do before then."

"But I hear your farm is immaculate as is. I'm sure we could hold it today, and everyone would be impressed."

That just proved to Charlotte how little this enthusiastic but misguided young lady really knew. If she had only seen their farm lately, before their usual spring cleaning, well . . .

"And you know how much of an honor it is to be selected Adams County Farm Family of the Year. You would be authorized to display the official Farm Family Foundation logo on any sort of sign you have for as long as you continue to own your farm."

"Official logo?"

"Oh yes. It's quite attractive really. Many of our agricultural operations use it as part of their marketing strategy."

"I see. Well, I don't know that we have a marketing strategy."

"That's all right. Just look at it this way: The recognition is just a matter of community pride. All your neighbors will tell you that."

Easy for Julie to say. She wouldn't have to paint the toolshed or the entire house, for that matter. What about all the fencing on the near corner of the North Quarter that needed fixing? Pete had left skeletal remains of a parts combine behind the barn; all that would have to be cleared up. Several rose beds would require serious spring weeding. And then she remembered the shingles over the north porch Bob had been promising to replace for the past five years . . .

"I'll need to talk to my husband," Charlotte finally managed to say.

"Yes, of course you do. You go right ahead and do that.

Meanwhile, I'll pencil you into the calendar, and could I hear back from you tonight?"

"*Tonight?*" Charlotte had a pretty good idea how Bob would react to this honor, never mind the prizes and the gift certificates. If she had been thinking straight, she would have just told this woman no right from the start.

"Right. That fellow at the *Leader* says he needs our flyers by tomorrow to insert in next week's paper. Otherwise we—"

"But the stickers with our names on them?"

"Oh. Right. Well, actually, we've already taken care of that."

"I see." Charlotte nodded. So things had already been decided. Probably all the churches and granges and youth groups had already been lined up. Her consent was just a formality. And Julie still sounded annoyingly perky on the other end of the line.

"I'll be sending a checklist to help you plan, Charlotte. And we'll chat again tonight, won't we? But let me be the first one to congratulate you on this wonderful honor. You and Robert will actually be the twenty-fifth Farm Family of the Year, so it's sort of a silver anniversary celebration."

"That's wonderful. So I'll . . . call you back tonight."

Charlotte hung up the phone feeling a bit numb at the way her to-do list had suddenly dropped to the floor as though weighed down with an impossible number of chores. She inhaled a warm cookie and then another before realizing what was in her mouth, but the chewing helped her think.

How could we ever do this? she asked herself. Right now,

three weeks might just as well have been three days. They couldn't get ready for an event like this, even if they all wanted to.

She did know at least one thing Julie Gauge had told her was true: Being selected as Farm Family of the Year was indeed a significant honor, even if they originally were the runners-up. People would come to the open house— hundreds usually did. The sign in the front lawn didn't matter a bit to her, and neither did the marketing logo. But the honor—now that was something else.

What's more, the kids might get a kick out of it, if for no other reason than they would find themselves part of an honored farm. Wouldn't that help them build their own pride, their own attachment to this land and the family tradition that had begun here generations ago? Wasn't that what Bob wanted? Perhaps she could talk him into accepting the honor after all.

She peeked out through the little window in the back door, still chewing a cookie and wondering as she watched her husband and son working together in the distance. How could they do this?

How could they not?

She placed three more cookies on a plate for the boys and reached once again for the doorknob, not noticing where Lightning had disappeared to. One step later, though, her yowl nearly sent Charlotte sprawling as she had apparently stepped on the end of the cat's tail.

"Lightning!" She hopped clear of the underfoot feline, dancing to the side and letting her out the door. Sometimes she wished they hadn't allowed Christopher to bring this barn cat inside, but it was obviously too late for that.

And now she paused on the back step, trying to make out a far and distant scent. Not the nutmeg or cloves from her plate of cookies, nor the touch of allspice that gave them a faint but pleasing kick. She breathed deeply, closing her eyes, and imagined Nebraska earth in April, rich and dark, turned to release the sweat and tears of generations— Bob and his father, his grandfather, each one coaxing their life from the dirt. The turning of the earth every year seemed to Charlotte to be a sort of holy ceremony, a prayer to God.

Speaking of which . . . Charlotte snapped open her eyes in recognition of the far-off scent, barely recognizable but still very certain. Not the teaspoon of vanilla she'd dropped into the cookie dough for good measure, though its rich hint might be mistaken for what she now knew to be rain.

So the weatherman had been right about his warnings, after all. It did not surprise her this time when she looked to the northwest to see a distant black line of clouds, high and billowing and angry—and coming straight for Heather Creek. Though the cold had not yet hit them in advance of the storm, she shivered at the thought of the now oncoming rain and hurried across the gravel to bring the men their cookies.

⌣ Chapter Three

A lmost as good as Mom's pies, huh?"

Pete stuffed the last of Charlotte's cookies into his mouth, which made it harder to understand him as he chewed. Charlotte would have told him to wipe his hands before he ate and to finish chewing before he spoke, but she had long since given up trying to correct her thirty-two-year-old son about anything, much less telling him how to eat. Her husband, Bob, on the other hand, nibbled half a cookie and returned to the plow they'd been repairing, tuning it up for the busy weeks to come.

"That your fifth one?" He grunted, picking up another wrench and locating something to tighten, and then looked over at his son as though they'd paused from their work quite long enough.

"Don't look at me." Pete held up a hand and took another bite. "Mom baked the applesauce kind for you special."

He looked over at Charlotte quickly with a word of apology. "Every bit as good as a cookie with sugar though, Mom. Thanks."

Toby had taken up her usual afternoon station at the end of the driveway, looking off toward Heather Creek

Road in anticipation of the kids' return from school. Once in a while the Australian shepherd/blue heeler cross would stand and wag her shaggy tail at a passing pickup or tractor, but then would sit back down. Her gaze never left the road as she focused on traffic that might be approaching from the direction of Bedford.

"I don't know how she knows," said Pete, enjoying the last bite of his cookie and checking his battered Timex. "But she knows."

"Wish my workers had as good a sense of time as the dog," mumbled Bob, but Pete hardly had a chance to protest as Toby began to bark at the sight of Sam's little old multicolored sports car. Or "sport scar," as Christopher described it.

The ancient vehicle Pete had received in trade for an odd job in town did carry more than its share of road scars. From a distance it reminded Charlotte of a muddy rainbow with splashes of primer gray, red, blue, and black. No telling what color it had been originally.

But even she had no trouble recognizing its distinct rusted-muffler roar as it bumped down the gravel driveway. Toby barked and wagged her tail wildly as Sam honked the horn. Charlotte thought if there ever were a good time to tell Bob about the phone call, it was now—with the kids around.

"Eat another one." She held out the plate to Bob. "They're for you, don't forget."

He really couldn't refuse, and eventually he stopped what he was doing long enough to pluck another cookie from the depleted pile. Then she waited until his mouth was full. With this kind of announcement, timing was everything.

"Got a call from a gal named Julie Gauge a little while ago." She made it sound as matter-of-fact as she knew how. "She said we were voted Farm Family of the Year."

Bob choked on his cookie, spraying crumbs all over his plow.

"Way to go, Mom." Pete sprang to his feet while Bob coughed. "I wouldn't have believed we had an in with the committee. What'd we win?"

"Well, she said there's a year's supply of butter, a fifty-dollar gift certificate from Home Depot, and a twenty-five-dollar gift certificate from Central Nebraska Veterinary Services."

"Woo-hoo!" Pete whooped. "That means we do the big fat open house too, huh?" He studied Charlotte a little more closely as Sam parked his car next to where they were talking. Then he smiled and held up a finger as if he'd just come up with the answer.

"Oh, wait a minute. I get it. April Fools', right? You've been waiting all day to say this. Waiting until the kids get home."

"Who's an April Fool?" Christopher popped out of the passenger seat, nearly knocking over his sister in the process. "Is Grandma doing an April Fool, the way she said she would?"

"It's no joke." Charlotte patted her husband on the back as he finished coughing, waiting for his face to return to its normal color. "What do you think, Bob?"

Bob shrugged away from her help and shook his head as

he went back to work on the plow. "You told them we'd do it, without asking me?"

"Not exactly. I said we'd get back to them. But they've already made many of the plans. So what do you think?"

"What do I think?" When he lowered his voice, Charlotte knew that generally meant trouble. "You know what I think about these kinds of things. I think, 'Pride goeth before destruction and a haughty spirit before a fall.'"

"Oh, come on, Bob. Who said anything about pride?"

He ignored her argument with a grunt, so she went on. "It's just a way for the community to take pride—er, to get together on someone's farm. You've been to them before."

"Once. Ten years ago. Didn't much care for all the hoopla and backslapping."

"Well, I don't know about backslapping. It's a celebration, plain and simple. You have to admit the prizes are nice. And we're not showing any pride by cleaning up the place and inviting people to come see."

"Inviting a *lot* of people," Pete said. But he didn't need to remind them.

"I think it sounds cool," Christopher volunteered. But Bob had dug in his heels, and he continued to shake his head. Charlotte wasn't done making her case though.

"It would be a good way for the kids to work together again," she said, "even if it's just in a small way. Remember how they worked together to bake pies last Thanksgiving?"

Finally Bob cleared his throat to give her an answer, of sorts. "I thought you wanted to forget that episode," he told her.

"They learned something from it. We all did."

"Maybe so. But I'm telling you, Charlotte, this thing is all about pride, and I don't want any part of it."

"Aw, Dad," Pete chimed in again. "That's really harsh. You're not actually serious, are you?"

"Even if I wasn't, you can guess how much money and how much work it takes to put on one of those things. Right now we don't have time for that."

"She said she would help us make most of the arrangements," Charlotte explained. "And—"

"And all we would have to do is clean the place up, right?" Bob waved his hand across the farm. "Even if I were of a mind to agree to this, you know I don't have time to be working all summer on cleanup. And who came up with this idea, anyway? Do they not know we actually have to work to make a living? Like we're just sitting around on the farm, waiting for something to do? Charlotte! We're setting up to plant, or don't the Farm Family folks know that?"

"They know." Charlotte wasn't sure she wanted to argue anymore, and her voice trailed off. "But it won't take all summer . . ."

Pete seemed to remember something, and he stepped back into the line of fire.

"Actually," he said, "I know when they had that thing at the Frasers' place, they were messing with cleanup projects for, well, it didn't take that long. Only a couple months. And our place is a little nicer than the Frasers', don't you think? We could probably have everything whipped into shape in—"

"It's in three weeks." Charlotte had to tell them now and let whatever happened, happen. Well, that shut them up.

Charlotte watched Pete's jaw drop and his face fall. Bob had obviously already made up his mind. Even the kids said nothing, though Charlotte guessed they had no idea what was going on. Finally Pete brightened.

"Three weeks, huh? That makes it easy."

"Easy?" Bob still couldn't believe it. "The planting, Pete. The planting. These people have no clue as to what is actually happening on an actual farm. They're idiots."

"Bob!" Charlotte wished she could cup her hands over Christopher's ears. "There's no need for that kind of talk."

"You know what he means, Mom." Pete turned back to his father. "But really, how much would it take to slap a coat of paint here and there? We do what we can do, and either way, we still get the prizes, right? Doesn't have to be perfect."

Charlotte marveled at how optimistic her son sounded—even if he didn't have a realistic view of the work it would take to make the farm presentable after this last winter.

"Besides," he said, "it's a huge honor, right? Afterward we get one of those fancy little signs we can plant in the front yard, like 'the Stevenson farm, since eighteen-whatever. Farm Family of the Year.' That would be worth the price of admission, right? I say we do it."

"No bragging. No sign. No." Bob shook his head again and went back to his repairs.

There would be no way around it if he was going to be this stubborn.

"It would be good for the kids." She tried one last gentle attempt to pry loose Bob's favor.

Pete clapped his hands. "That's it!" he cried, pointing to Christopher. "I'll get the kids to help me, and we'll do it ourselves. You won't have to do anything, Dad."

Sam and Emily must have figured out the gist of what was being discussed by now and were drifting off toward the house, backpacks and schoolbooks in hand. Surely they realized this would mean more work.

"I have one word for you, Pete." Bob didn't appear to be loosening his position at all as he tightened down a nut. But that wasn't dampening Pete's spirits in the least. "And it's the same one as before: planting."

"Don't worry about it, Dad. Honestly. We'll get the planting done, and we'll get the cleanup done too. It's not every day you get honored as Farm Family of the Year. Just think, we're going to be on the news and in the paper, probably in the Nebraska State Grange newsletter. What more can you ask for?"

Again, that was probably the wrong approach to take with Bob. His face clouded even more, if that were possible.

"That's exactly what I'm talking about."

"So you don't have any objection if we do all the work?" asked Pete. Charlotte gave him credit for not giving up.

Bob grunted again, and he worked his mouth the way he did when he was not at all pleased. His hand slipped on the wrench.

"Look," he said, "all I'm saying is, we don't have time for this kind of foolishness, and I don't think it would be a good idea, even if we did have the time. But you do what you want to do."

By his detachment Charlotte could tell he had conceded. But this wasn't exactly what she'd had in mind. Now, though, there was no stopping Pete as he gathered and recruited the kids.

"Good! We're going to take care of this, Mom." He turned back with a smile, and Bob's shoulders fell.

"Planting," he mumbled, but he said nothing more as he glanced up at the approaching line of clouds. He would be able to smell the rain every bit as much as Charlotte could.

And the dark, worried look on his face did nothing to comfort her.

"CHARLOTTE DEAR! I am so excited for you!" When Charlotte's best friend, Hannah Carter, smiled, her entire face lit up. She stopped in the middle of Heather Creek Road, halfway through their after-supper walk. "And I'll tell you this: no one deserves the honor more than you do."

"Thanks for the vote of confidence, but . . ." Charlotte tried to keep up with Hannah as they turned and headed west toward the setting sun peeking through dark clouds. They walked together past fields bursting with promise and smelling of newly turned earth. A pair of noisy robins flittered past, just overhead.

"But what?" asked Hannah. "Is there a problem?"

The slimmer and younger Hannah could easily outpace Charlotte if she wanted to. Never mind the gray-tinged blonde hair; in her perky white running shoes and mismatched blue and gold sweats she looked rather athletic and ready to run. But she held back and studied her friend, concern written on her face.

"Well, I don't know what to call it, exactly." Charlotte

wasn't sure how to explain without sounding as if she were painting Bob in a bad light, so she chose her words carefully. "The problem is, I'm not so sure it's going to be a big hit with . . . you know, everyone." There. She'd said it.

With the concern of a friend who knew when something wasn't quite right, Hannah waited for Charlotte to explain.

"Bob believes it's about pride," said Charlotte. Then she added quickly, "And I completely respect his point of view. It could easily turn into something like that if we aren't careful."

"I understand."

"But . . . on the other hand, I really think it would be good for us as a family. Pete said he would help, and the kids will all pitch in too."

"The way they did when you baked all those pies last Thanksgiving?"

Charlotte had to smile at the gentle reminder of last fall's fiasco.

"All right. I have to admit that topic did come up."

Hannah nodded as if she understood. But then, Hannah always understood. She again waited patiently for Charlotte to explain herself a little more.

"I also thought doing the open house sounded like a good opportunity to affirm the kids, so maybe they'll feel part of something bigger than themselves. I just don't want it to be, you know, an issue with Bob."

"You think it will be?" Hannah rested a friendly arm around Charlotte's shoulder as they continued on, and it warmed her in the cooling of the early evening. They would have to get home soon.

"I hope not. But he was pretty adamant, as you can imagine."

By that time she knew she'd said enough—perhaps more than enough. So they walked on in silence, now several feet from each other but very much in step. Minutes later Hannah looked up at the darkening sky. Soon the first star would make an appearance—maybe the North Star or a bright planet. But not just yet.

"Ring around the moon," said Hannah, recalling the farmers' verse, "means rain or snow upon us soon."

Charlotte shivered at the thought of bitter weather ahead, but even more at the thought of Bob's disapproval. For the moment, however, all she could do was pull up the collar of her jacket. They headed back the way they came, a little faster now.

Chapter
Four

Cup of coffee, Bob?"

Brad Weber motioned to a gurgling Mister Coffee at the end of the cluttered counter at AA Tractor Supply, just behind a huge parts catalog mounted on a large swivel stand. It almost reminded Bob of the way Pastor Evans had mounted a large Bible on the Communion table in the front of their church. The Bible had belonged to Bob's great-grandfather, one of the church's charter members in 1904.

But this was a very different kind of sanctuary, where farmers came in during the early morning to swap testimonies and compare notes about the latest fertilizer or find out what kind of repair their equipment might need. Or, like Bob, they came to pick up a part for a broken-down piece of old farm machinery. Then, from behind the counter, Brad and his father, Andy, would pass out their own variety of Communion cups—in this case, coffee mugs—before the farmers returned to the planting, or the harvest, or the latest job at hand.

Bob wouldn't admit it out loud, but he could think of no better place to start the seventh day of the week, and no more comforting sound than the tinkle of doorbells announcing his arrival in the parts sanctuary.

"Sure, coffee." Bob nodded, careful not to say too much too soon. One- or two-word answers were preferred here, at least until the coffee was poured. "Thanks."

He plucked his faded blue mug from the row of pegs above the coffee machine and poured himself a cup, the same way he had done for years, even before Brad's dad came down with Parkinson's and had to pull back from the business. Andy might still be shuffling around in the maze of tall shelves behind the counter, where the parts were stored, but Brad was the face now behind the cash register.

"Good coffee." Bob took a sip of the plain black Folgers. None of that fancy flavored stuff that jetted out of noisy stainless steel machines. Here, hot was the main ingredient, and the best brew remained unadorned.

"Yeah, just as fresh as when I brewed that pot last week." Brad kept a straight face and leaned across the counter. "So what can I do for you on this bee-*yoo*-tiful Saturday morning?"

Bob reached into the pocket of his weathered jeans and pulled out what was left of a twisted piece of metal, the green paint mostly worn off. Time for a test. He would see if the young Brad would recognize it.

"Need one of these," Bob replied. "Come off a—"

"John Deere 7000 planter, narrow." Brad finished Bob's sentence with a small grin as he snatched the ruined part from Bob's hand and turned it around in his own. "I know what you and Pete run out there."

Of course he did. Brad knew every piece of major equipment run by every farmer in a fifty-mile radius, and then some. Buy a new piece, and Brad was the first to know. Trade an older piece, and Brad would find that out as well.

"Think I got one of 'em. Older model, but that part's the same."

"Right." Bob took another sip as Brad disappeared back into the maze to find the replacement.

"Still feel bad about your grandson, by the way," Brad called back from somewhere behind the shelves. "I thought he could be a good worker. He gonna help you with this year's crop?"

"Yeah, thanks. Still in school, you know. He's learned a lot though. Maybe he could get another chance here sometime. Maybe . . ." Bob didn't know how to finish. *Maybe what?* The thought of Sam helping him and Pete on the farm full-time had never really crossed his mind. In fact, it was the last thing he imagined possible, though he couldn't help wishing. What would it take to get a kid like that interested in an operation like theirs?

The doorbells jingled again as a couple more farmers entered. At this time of the morning Bob knew even before turning to look that it would be Mutt and Jeff, also known as his neighbors Frank Carter and Paul Hubbard.

Nobody was sure how long the two farmers had been friends—probably since grade school. They had become closer since Paul's wife, Sandy, died years ago. But what an odd couple: Frank was every bit as lanky as Paul was short and round. Frank wore the spring sun in tanned stripes across his face while Paul looked red and burned even in the dead of winter.

"If it ain't Early Bird Stevenson," said Paul as Bob turned to nod his good morning. "You going to mud-in your corn again this year?"

"You know I've never done that." Bob could take a little good-natured ribbing for his habit of being one of the first in the county to plant. He would have most of his crop in the ground by the end of the month while some of his neighbors preferred to wait, even until early May. But waiting, he thought, was even riskier than not.

"You know we just give you a hard time," Frank put in as he sauntered up to the counter. "Everybody else in the county would like to get the yield you and Pete do. I don't know how you manage. Brad, how does this gentleman keep outproducing all the rest of us year after year?"

"Secret formula." Bob took another sip to hide a smile.

"Yeah, so it's about time they gave you the Farm Family of the Year award." Frank laid his hand-scrawled shopping list on the counter and waited his turn. He must have noticed Bob's less-than-enthusiastic response. "Though I gotta say I wouldn't wish it on my best friend, with all the work you're going to have to do now. You can quote me on this: Them women will have you a honey-do list longer than your arm, wait and see. And with planting coming up . . ."

"Hey, hold on." Bob sputtered on his coffee. "Who said anything about us being Farm Family of the Year?"

"You mean it's still a secret?" Paul pulled up to the counter with the other two, plunking down a small box of grease-crusted parts that apparently needed replacing. Brad would have fun with it. "I heard Sally Meyers last night at the market telling everybody who would listen. Hey, this is a big event, you know."

"*Hmm.*" Though it didn't surprise Bob that the Herko's clerk felt free to spread the news, that would have been before Charlotte even called Julie Gauge back with their decision. But of course most news traveled around town faster than Rick Barnes at the *Leader* could keep up with it.

"So here's your part." Brad returned and plunked the shiny green tractor part down on the counter. "I gave you an extra set-screw; you'll probably be needing it, especially if you're planning to run through damp soil."

Once again Bob had to defend himself against the critics. "I can wait till it's all dried out; you know that. Just can't afford to wait into May, or my yields dip way down. Am I right?"

He returned his cup to the rack and nodded his thanks. He'd had enough of this discussion, especially as it had to do with the Farm Family nonsense. Which only reminded him of the way he and Charlotte had disagreed about the matter, and that made his stomach turn downright sour. He could handle just about anything, he thought, with Charlotte on his side. But when they were at odds, well, that changed everything.

"Let us know if you need help with the cleanup list," added Frank, chuckling. Bob wasn't entirely sure how serious he was. Even in the best of times, he assumed Hannah gave Frank a lengthy list of his own. So what was he grinning about?

"Yeah, and stay dry," said Brad, pointing out the shop window. Things had changed even in the short time since Bob had stepped into the parts store. By now there could be no mistaking the stampede of angry black clouds that hovered overhead.

"Farm Fool of the Year." He kicked at a discarded gum wrapper in the gutter, wishing it would all go away, wishing he had stood up to the idea more strongly, right from the start. Nothing good could come of thumbing one's nose at Scripture.

I'm sorry, God. He shot up a prayer as he hurried along. *I should have stopped it when I had a chance.*

And as he hurried to his truck he instinctively raised an arm against the cold rain that in moments would turn Lincoln Street into a river. Oh, he'd known it was coming, all right. Just not so soon and so fast. Soaked in the downpour, he ran for the truck.

BACK AT THE HOUSE, Charlotte looked out the living room window to see how the sky could have darkened so quickly. At least it matched her mood. When Bob had left earlier this morning—without saying anything to her—she'd noticed a distant sun still trying gamely to peek through. Now sheets of serious rain made it difficult to even see across the yard to the barn, and water was over the edge of the roof, overpowering any gutter's ability to keep up.

Let it rain, she thought, crossing her arms to her chest and wondering how the good news about being chosen as

Farm Family of the Year could have turned so bad. *I should never have pushed the issue.*

Good thing they'd avoided an even more serious thunderstorm, or lightning, or even a tornado—so far. But she couldn't be sure. So she flipped on the TV in the family room to hear if the forecaster could tell them something new.

". . . but we're tracking a large system from the Gulf that promises to bring plenty of moisture to southeast Nebraska. Details after the sports report."

Charlotte didn't care too much about the sports report but turned up the volume anyway. Maybe the noise would help take her mind off her argument with Bob. After a brief basketball recap and a shampoo commercial, the local weatherman appeared on the screen in front of a large Nebraska map tattooed with moving lines and computer-drawn cloud and rain symbols.

"As we reported at the top of the hour," he said, "we're experiencing a new band of storms from the Southeast, bringing heavy precipitation to central and south-central Nebraska, with reports of minor flooding and hail damage in parts of Nuckolls, Webster, and Adams counties."

Now he paced from side to side, motioning toward different parts of his map. "But the really bad news isn't even here yet, as there appears to be no letup in sight. Every indication is that we have at least a week of the same in store for us, with a kind of 'perfect-storm' system pushing up from the East this way, and then the moisture creeping in from the South the way you see in the Storm Tracker map. Looks like farmers can forget about the early planting they'd been hoping for. Most are going to be delayed by several weeks."

Funny he should say that. Omaha stations rarely reported anything of real interest to farmers, but this storm system clearly had the weatherman concerned. And he'd be a little more concerned if he could see the weather for himself as it descended on Heather Creek Farm—now wave after wave of nearly solid water, pinging on the picture window and splattering mud in all directions from the flower beds around the house.

"There go my marigolds." Charlotte could only watch helplessly as the rain disassembled the pretty yellow annuals she'd planted just the other day—too early, as it turned out. Purple and red pansies were pretty much history beneath the heavy showers as well. Even Lightning woke up from her nap on the flowered sofa to take notice.

"Maybe I deserve it, Lightning." The cat began to purr as Charlotte stroked her head. "But what am I supposed to do, go out there with an umbrella and stand over all my plants?"

She might even have done so if a truck hadn't turned into the driveway just then. Through the pouring rain, Charlotte could hardly tell who it was until the driver had splashed his way through massive puddles to pull into the gravel parking area behind the house. A moment later Bob came bursting into the house, shaking out his clothes like Toby after a bath.

"You're back!" Charlotte almost gave him a big hug but thought better of it. Better to smooth things over first.

"Almost didn't make it through the runoff," he said,

mopping a strand of gray hair off his forehead. "Culvert must have already backed up. The water covered Heather Creek Road like a lake."

"And you were out there driving in it?" Images of newscasts showing flooded-out vehicles with water up to their roofs came to mind, a scenario Charlotte had once seen on a weather-disaster television special. What if it had been Bob? "What would you have done if you'd gotten stuck?"

"I didn't."

"Yes, but you just said it was bad. The kids are always talking about their cell phones. Maybe it's time we got you one."

"Me? Ha! It's just one more thing to pay for each month. That, on top of all the stuff you think you're going to buy for that open house thing."

"I'm not buying a lot of things. I told you that."

She didn't like the way her voice seemed to sharpen when she got emotional. But whose fault was it for bringing that up again anyway?

"Hmph." Bob crossed his arms, obviously not backing down. "You know how much one of those cell things costs?"

"I have no idea. But if we're talking about you getting stuck, how much would that cost? It would be worth it."

"We're not talking about me getting stuck, and it would not be worth it." He raised his voice in a way that signaled he was done with this conversation.

Only problem was, Charlotte wasn't. "I'm going to find out how much a phone for you would cost."

"Don't know why you'd waste your time."

"What?" She couldn't believe it.

"Look." He held up his hands. "I'm sorry. But I don't need a cell phone and I don't want to waste more time talking about it. Now . . . I forget what I came in here for."

Thinking she heard a noise on the stairs, Charlotte glanced at the TV, now muted but still featuring the earnest young weatherman gesturing at weather graphics. Despite how angry she'd felt just a moment ago, it reminded her of what had set off this argument in the first place.

"Bob, I didn't mean to get so upset. I just didn't want you to, you know . . ." Charlotte didn't quite know how to finish her thought, but her husband must have read her discomfort. He softened as he snapped off the TV.

"Don't worry about me." He headed for the bathroom. "It might rain for the next year, but I float."

Somehow that didn't comfort her much. And the sound of footsteps going back up the stairs told her that someone had been listening in on their argument.

Chapter Five

Maybe it wouldn't rain for a whole year straight, as Bob had said. But it started to feel that way to Charlotte over the next several days, with nearly unbroken showers Monday, then Tuesday and Wednesday . . . and beyond.

When she woke up to even more rain the next Sunday morning Charlotte thought she'd better supply the family with plenty of breakfast, and extra-early. They might need extra time for the drive to church if the highways had flooded again. Perhaps the road wouldn't even be passable. She glanced over at Bob as he snored and couldn't help thinking of a silly bumper sticker she'd once seen:

SOMETIMES I WAKE UP GRUMPY . . . AND SOMETIMES I LET HIM SLEEP.

So she let Bob sleep and stepped quietly out of her room to the kitchen, startling Christopher in the process. "Whatever are you doing with that plastic cup, Christopher?"

From where he huddled over something at the kitchen table, he nearly jumped out of his Spiderman pajamas, sending a ruler and a cup clattering to the floor.

"Grandma!" His eyes widened even more as he whirled around. "You scared me."

"I'm sorry, dear. I thought you heard me coming."

She helped him pick his project off the floor, though Christopher appeared clearly sheepish and tucked away the marker in his hand when she picked up the blue translucent tumbler. There was no mistaking the little lines and numbers he'd carefully marked along the side of the cup from top to bottom. She held it up to him in a silent question.

"I didn't think anyone would mind." He avoided her eyes. "It's not one you care about, is it?"

"You really should have asked, Christopher, before marking on it." She looked at the cup. "But I suppose this one was sort of cracked on the top. So what kind of measuring cup are you making here?"

He brightened at the question. "I'm making my own weather station. Directions were in the book I got for Christmas. This is going to be the rain gauge, and then I'm going to make a wind-speed measurer. An anemometer. Plus a barometer to measure atmospheric pressure. You know, in millibars."

"Millibars. Naturally." She eyed his work a little more closely, noting his careful lines and neat numbers before handing it back. "I'm just impressed that you know all those big words, and even know what they mean. You do know what they mean?"

"It's not so hard." He shrugged. "Miss Rivkin helped me find some books at the library on how to be a meteorologist. That's what I'm going to be, you know."

"Yes, I know." She smiled. How many times had he told them? "And you need this cup to measure what, exactly?"

"Rainfall, of course." He pointed to the lines for her. "See, each line is a tenth of an inch, so when I put it outside, we can know how much it rained in the past twenty-four hours, and I can tell Mr. Barnes at the newspaper."

"Mr. Barnes? Really?"

"He said he might print what I tell him about the weather, because the only stuff he can get is all the way from Harding, and that's not as good."

"You spoke with him yourself?"

"He came to school the other day to take some pictures of students of the month. I asked him."

Charlotte nodded at her grandson's initiative, glad he'd found a project that interested him so much. Now if only he could learn to ask before commandeering one of her plastic cups. "We'll just need to find a good place outside for this cup," she told him.

A few minutes later she had bundled up in Bob's black rain slicker and slipped her stocking feet into his enormous boots, while Christopher tripped alongside her wearing his own hooded orange raincoat. Outside, the wind whipped at her hair and drove a cold drizzle into her face, but the back-porch light helped them see their way in the early morning darkness. Talk about April showers! Even so, Toby must have seen them coming. She came running in their direction from the barn, braving the rain.

"Here!" Christopher decided, placing his new rain gauge on the ground at the edge of the driveway, away from trees and just out of reach of potential traffic. He wedged several larger rocks around the cup to keep it from falling or being blown over, and stood back to admire his work while Charlotte did her best to keep the rain from dribbling down her back. Toby inspected everything with a thorough sniff.

"It's nothing for you, girl," Charlotte told her, and the dog looked back up at her with a wag of her tail.

"So now I just check it again in twenty-four hours," he said, "and then I can call Mr. Barnes, right?"

By that time Charlotte had already turned back to get under cover.

"Why don't you come in now and get some breakfast?" she asked. "You're going to have plenty of time to get wet in this weather, especially if it keeps up this way. And you'll have plenty of time to collect rain too. But right now we just need to see about collecting the others for church."

He watched the rain splashing into his gauge for a few more moments before joining her back inside.

"Grandma?" asked Christopher as he peeled off his wet coat and hung it on a tree by the door. Rainwater pooled on the linoleum around him. "There's one more thing I wanted to do, actually."

She waited for him to go on as she pulled a bowl of fresh eggs and a pitcher of milk from the refrigerator. "What one thing did you want to do?" she asked.

"Well, Sam said the water in the creek is getting a lot higher."

She stopped cold, a mixing bowl in her hand. "You are most definitely not going anywhere near the creek right now," she told him, lowering her voice in warning and making sure she kept it in check. Christopher looked up at her and started to say something, but she wasn't finished.

"Especially not now," she told him. "Do you understand what I'm saying?"

"I understand, Grandma. I was just thinking that if Sam could help me, or maybe even Grandpa, then we could sink a big long stick in the creek and keep track of how high it was getting. I could mark it, the way I marked my rain gauge, and then we could—"

"No, no, no." She shook her head with nearly enough force to dislocate her neck. "Absolutely not."

"Huh?" He didn't seem to get it. "Why not?"

"First of all, it's far too dangerous to be anywhere near the creek right now." She counted off the most obvious reasons on her fingers. "And second of all, you're not going to let your grandfather do that kind of thing either. He's been under a lot of stress lately, with planting coming up. And now this weather."

"And the Farm Family of the Year thing he doesn't want us to do?"

"It's not that he doesn't want us to do it." She tried to make her voice sound calm and reassuring once more. "It's just that . . ."

Her voice trailed off, caught in the tangle of what they both knew to be so: that Bob didn't want them to do it, period. He had his reasons, however narrow or ill-advised she privately thought them to be. But there really was no getting around the fact.

"It's just that he has a lot on his mind this time of year." She finished her sentence as kindly as she knew how.

"Is that why he was yelling at you yesterday?"

"Yelling at me? When did you—oh, honey, I don't want you to think Grandpa was yelling at me."

"But he was. I heard it. Mom used to yell like that sometimes."

"I hope not too often."

"Well, no. But you act like you're mad at each other all the time. You both sounded mad. And you were slamming stuff around."

Charlotte swallowed hard, wondering how close he had come to the truth. Were they really mad at each other all the time? Surely not.

"Oh dear. Well, whatever you heard, it wasn't yelling." She checked her words carefully. "I was just concerned about him driving around in a flood, and he was just being . . . well, you know how Grandpa can get."

"Yeah . . ."

"I suppose he's just a little stubborn sometimes. Or maybe *determined* is a better word. That can be a good thing, you know."

"It didn't sound like a good thing to me. He just sounded like he was yelling."

"Well, he wasn't. He was trying to make his point."

"Then you don't think he would yell at me if I asked him to help with the flood measuring stick?"

Talk about determined! Christopher may have picked up that quality from his grandfather, if it was the sort of genetic trait that could be passed along. Charlotte sighed and patted Christopher's shoulder, catching his gaze.

"Listen to me, Christopher. Grandpa wouldn't yell at you, and he's not mad at you for any reason."

"You're sure about that?"

"Positive. But I don't want you to mention it to him. I don't want you to even ask him. Okay?"

"Oh." Christopher's face fell. "Not even if—"

"What are we not asking me?" Bob shuffled into the kitchen without warning, scratching the day-old stubble on his chin and hitching up his jeans. Charlotte couldn't say she was thrilled with his timing, and she quickly turned to crack eggs into her bowl as if she hadn't heard his question.

"Scrambled okay with you this morning?" she asked with a touch of added cheer. With a bowlful of scrambled eggs, they could serve themselves as much as they liked, and then some.

Thankfully Bob didn't press the issue or repeat his question. He just gave them a quizzical look as he lowered himself into a chair and poured himself a glass of orange juice.

"Long as they're not too dry."

Which, despite the cholesterol, was okay on her account —as long as Christopher dropped the topic of measuring the creek. She gave him a quick warning look, and over the next several minutes he told his grandfather all about the rain gauge and his plans for building some of the other weather instruments. This, apparently, was what meteorologists did.

Charlotte kept track of their conversation from her spot in front of the stove, and from where she stood it all seemed quite sweet. After all, how often did Christopher and his grandfather have a chance to just sit and chat on an early Sunday morning without Sam or Emily interrupting? She finished the eggs, scooped them into a bowl, and set them on the table.

"You really want to be a weatherman, eh?" Bob asked a few minutes later.

"*Meteorologist*, Grandpa. You know, they get to be on TV, and they get to use a lot of cool computer games."

"*Hmm*. Still sounds to me like a fancy name for a weatherman. *Meteorologist*. Okay, then, what do they do, study meteors?"

Christopher wrinkled his nose, obviously not recognizing his grandfather's attempt at humor.

"I don't know too much about meteors," Christopher replied. "All I know is, I'm going to be the guy on the TV telling people when it's going to rain and snow and stuff. Only difference is, I'm going to be right."

"Okay, then." Bob considered another bite of eggs, sprinkling another dash of pepper over his plate. "You go right ahead and dream big. But that means you've got to get good grades, especially in math and science. Doesn't it?"

Again Christopher wrinkled his nose, as if he hadn't considered such a thing.

"I do okay, Grandpa."

Bob winked at him.

"I'm just giving you a hard time. So what's the outlook today, Mr. Meteorologist?"

With great aplomb, Christopher walked over to the back door, opening it slightly. After poking his hand outside for a moment, he brought it back inside—dripping wet.

"Rain today," he announced in a deep voice, and that was enough to make Grandpa chuckle. Problem was, the "rain today" also brought Pete tumbling in with it, and he hit the still-open back door hard enough to send it slamming back into the kitchen wall. Christopher jumped out of the way just in time to avoid being flattened while a wet Toby slipped in behind him.

"Good-night, Pete!" Bob dropped his fork as he rose to his feet. "You don't have to break the door down. What's gotten into you?"

"Sorry, but—" Pete was surely on a mission, and he stood there, dripping for a moment and panting. Mud covered his boots and caked his jeans. He wore a ripped black windbreaker, which unfortunately hadn't shielded him much from the weather, and his dark brown hair stuck out at random angles from underneath a greasy red and white Nebraska Huskers baseball cap. The cap apparently hadn't shielded him much from the weather either.

"Creek's going to flood anytime," he announced. "You've got to see it!"

Charlotte should not have been surprised at his remark, as Pete still had a knack for saying the wrong thing at precisely the wrong time. Before she could stop anyone, all three headed for the door to investigate, Toby at their heels.

"Wait for me!" Christopher grabbed his wet coat again

and stepped on his uncle's heels on the way out. And yes, he still wore his Spiderman pajamas underneath.

"You can't go out there in that rain, Christopher," Charlotte said to the door that slammed in her face. "Not like that!"

Chapter
Six

L ater that afternoon Emily looked out the passenger-side window of Charlotte's blue Ford and pointed toward the swollen river as they drove over the little bridge a few miles down Heather Creek Road from the farm. Much higher, and it would be flooding the roadway.

"I still can't believe he lost his boot in the mud like that," she told her grandma. "Do you think it was just some kind of guy thing, that they had to go out there, or what?"

Charlotte kept her eyes glued to the road and gripped the steering wheel until she thought it might break. Just because the rain had momentarily let up since church ended didn't mean they still might not run into trouble. After all, the sky to the south appeared definitely ominous, dark gray and overcast with clouds that seemed even more pregnant with moisture. She told herself they could turn around anytime, or at the first sign of trouble, or if they encountered any floodwaters threatening the road.

"Grandma?"

"Oh yes. Sure. A guy thing. I suppose you could call it that. I didn't like them going out there either."

"Yeah, I mean, it absolutely drives me crazy when Sam and Christopher are, like, poking sticks in bonfires, or like this morning, when they think they have to be all macho and get right up next to where it was about to flood, you know, just because. Sam told me the water was washing tree branches and stuff down the creek, and it was all gross and muddy. And then Christopher had this crazy idea he was telling me about putting a big stick in the creek, so they could tell how high the water was getting. I mean, hello? I think we know when water starts coming over the edge or, like, flooding the kitchen floor, don't we? Do you need a stick to tell you that? I don't need a stick."

After a short while Charlotte relaxed just a little, and as they drew closer to Harding they chatted about other things on the farm and how silly Emily's brothers sometimes acted. Fortunately, thought Charlotte, they still had encountered no disasters on the road, and no floods. Yet.

See? she told herself. *We girls can handle this.* She let her granddaughter continue. A ride in the car always seemed to provide a good opportunity to connect. Maybe they had a little more in common than she'd thought. But when they hit a large puddle the little car shuddered and even rose off the pavement a bit as spray flew out to both sides.

"That's not good." Charlotte slowed way down and considered pulling over to the side of the road, but Emily urged her on.

"We're okay, Grandma." She must have noticed Charlotte's white knuckles on the steering wheel. "Just a little puddle."

Actually it was more than just a little puddle, but it was

probably too late now to turn back as they passed a sign that said Harding was just 3.5 miles away. So Charlotte took a deep breath and forced herself not to panic while her mind returned to the task at hand. Why was she getting so nervous anyway about a little rain on the road? Emily went on, and still it seemed she didn't mind talking with her grandmother, for once. Charlotte knew she should take advantage of the situation.

"So I'm thinking I should invite Ashley, of course, but there're a few other girls from school I can probably ask too. Not Nicole Evans though; she's so stuck up. If I ask her, some of the others might not come. Do you think ten would be too many? We could do makeovers. And I was thinking maybe a sleepover might be fun."

The question caught Charlotte momentarily off guard, and she turned to Emily.

"Wait a moment. We're not talking about missing boots in the mud anymore, are we?"

"Grandma." Emily frowned with the kind of look that Charlotte feared—the teen "you *so* don't understand" look.

Unfortunately, Charlotte *so* didn't understand.

"I'm sorry." Charlotte did her best to wrestle the derailed conversation back on track. "My mind was somewhere else. Tell me what you were saying again."

Emily's rolled eyes told Charlotte her chances for reconnecting had moved from slim to none.

"My birthday coming up next Sunday? The party you said I could have? You weren't even listening."

Now Emily's voice dripped with the same kind of irritation Charlotte's daughter Denise used to display so often, before she ran away. Though it had been nearly seventeen years, Charlotte could remember it as if it were only this morning. And yes, this situation was just like those she'd had with Denise, all over again, and nothing Charlotte said now would be able to change it.

"I'm sorry, Emily. Please go ahead. What were you saying about the party?"

"Forget it. You and Grandpa don't want me to have the party anyway."

"Why would you say that? Of course we do. I'm just not sure if what you're thinking is what we were thinking. I don't know if you understand what kind of money we can spend on something like this."

"I said forget it." Emily crossed her arms across her chest and swiveled toward the side window, cutting off any chance of conversation until they pulled up in the soggy parking lot of the Harding Garden Center. Charlotte turned off the car and set the parking brake; she hesitated a moment before pulling her list from her purse. This was, after all, the reason they'd driven all this way through the inclement weather.

"Okay, so you're going to help me pick out the flowers for the yard, right?" She tried to sound cheery, as if nothing had happened in the car. Maybe Emily would brighten up and forget all about it. "We have to make sure we have enough color for the open house, you know."

"Whatever." But Emily didn't move or uncross her arms. This grandmother-granddaughter excursion to buy flowers hadn't turned out quite the way she'd hoped. On the other hand, Emily did eventually consent to following Charlotte around the garden center, sometimes at a distance, though she looked away sullenly whenever Charlotte asked her opinion about begonias, marigolds, or pansies.

"What about these?" Charlotte steered their cart, now laden with flats of colorful bedding plants, and pointed toward a beautiful display of red and white geraniums.

I'm going to scream if Emily says "whatever" one more time! she thought.

Fortunately Emily displayed a slightly enlarged vocabulary and mumbled something about red and white flowers looking lame next to the house. Charlotte wasn't sure exactly what that meant, or how Emily had come to that conclusion, but she appreciated the attempt.

"*Hmm.*" Charlotte nodded her head and stroked her chin with what she hoped was an appropriate measure of thoughtfulness. "I think maybe you're right, Emily. They would look terribly lame. We'll get something else."

"Really?" Emily looked surprised, and her ice seemed to thaw a few degrees as they continued on through the aisles of the nursery, past piles of fertilizer and grass seed, fruit trees and pretty blooming bushes like azaleas and rhododendrons. Even so, Emily frowned at the cartload of color, and at Charlotte's list.

"Yeah, but I still don't understand why you think you need to plant so many flowers all over the place," she said. "Why does everything have to be so . . . perfect? The flowers all just die anyway."

"You don't like the flowers? I thought you liked flowers. Isn't that why you came with me?"

Emily sighed again and looked away. "Sure, they're okay. Fine. I mean, forget it."

Once again, Charlotte didn't understand. She had no idea now how to answer her granddaughter's objections, or even what they really were. But with or without Emily's help, they eventually decided on another flat of marigolds—some of Charlotte's favorites—and some delightful cosmos and African daisies. The young clerk in a green apron smiled broadly at them as she pointed her handheld checkout scanner at each little barcode.

"Oh, these are going to look gorgeous in your yard," she gushed, looking straight at Emily as if she knew her personally. "Did you pick them out?"

Emily seemed to catch her breath, and then let her shoulders droop as she nodded. "Some of them," she admitted.

"I just don't know when we're going to be able to plant anything," the clerk went on, ringing up a total. "What with all this rain, everything's just turning to mud. Terrible. Are you girls local?"

"Bedford," Charlotte explained, and the clerk nodded knowingly as she explained that her cousin lived in Bedford, and that all the creeks were rising there.

Normally Charlotte would have asked the name of the gal's cousin since she likely would have known the person, or at least would recognize the name. This time, however, she just let the clerk replace the plants in their cart.

"In fact," added the clerk, looking up through an overhead lattice, "I heard a forecast that said we're going to see at least another week of rain."

She handed Charlotte the receipt with a smile. "But you girls have a wonderful rest of your Sunday."

Charlotte nodded her thanks and wheeled their cart as quickly as she could back to the car. Maybe they could outrun the advancing storm. A little boy with a cart full of bagged landscaping bark nearly collided with her as heavy drops of rain began to splatter the pavement. The storm gathered strength and turned once again into a downpour. All in less than a minute.

"Don't look now, Grandma," said Emily as they loaded plants into the trunk, "but it's starting to rain again."

Yes it was. The question was, for how long? She looked at her list again, now soggy from the rain and barely readable. Maybe it didn't matter. She crumpled it and stuffed it into her purse as they climbed back into the car.

Chapter Seven

Christopher?"

Miss Rivkin waved at him as the rest of her fifth-grade class pulled on raincoats and gathered up their backpacks at the end of the school day on Monday. "Could I ask you something before you leave, please?"

Christopher hesitated as his friend Dylan brushed by him.

"Oooo," Dylan teased him in a low voice. "You're in trouble."

"Am not." But Christopher couldn't be sure, and his mind raced to remember anything he might have said, done, or not done to make the teacher call him aside. He stuffed his drawing notebook and his reading book, *A Way Through the Sea*, into his backpack and cautiously approached the front desk while Dylan waved from the door.

"Gotta catch my bus," Dylan told him. "See ya."

Christopher waved back and paused in front of their teacher, wondering.

"Don't worry." Miss Rivkin smiled at him and put down her assignment book. "You're not in trouble."

"Oh." He breathed a little easier, waiting for her to explain.

"It's about your weather station."

How did she know? He hadn't told her anything about it yet.

"I heard some of the kids talking about it. Am I right? You're thinking of building a weather station for your science project?"

"Well, yeah." He explained to her what he had already done, and what he hoped to do. She nodded and leaned a little closer.

"That's fantastic, Christopher. Between you and me, I don't have many students who are quite so ambitious. So you just came up with the idea on your own?"

"I'm going to be a meteorologist," he told her, and he assumed he would not have to explain what the word meant.

"I have no doubt about that, especially after the wonderful tornado report you wrote last fall, and now this."

He would be on TV someday, telling people about the weather. They would see. But right now, he worried that everybody would think his rain gauge and all the other things were stupid. Maybe a sixth grader would do the same thing as him, only a lot better. And then what would people say? He could hear them laughing already.

"Well, if you need any help," she said, "you just let me know. I have some good books on the subject. And remember, it's due at the end of the month."

Christopher nodded so she would let him go. He headed for the door.

"Sure, Miss Rivkin." He tried to sound polite. "But if I don't hurry, my brother's going to leave for home without me."

Which actually was true, though it hadn't quite happened yet. But last week Sam had almost pulled out of the high school parking lot in his old piece-of-junk car and Christopher had to wave him down. Today felt even later than that.

He hurried through the after-school crowds in the hallway, knocking elbows with several kids and nearly slipping on wet floors near the school's main entry. Just outside the doors, teachers tried to keep a lid on the confusion of kids, cars, buses, and rain, but a cold shower pounded so loudly on the roof overhead that everyone had to yell to be heard. That made things worse.

Christopher ran by the water-logged crossing guard, trying to avoid the bigger puddles, but he felt the rain soaking through to his socks. Sam would be leaving without him, for sure.

"Wait for me!" Christopher whispered as he ran over to the high school parking lot. He mopped the rain from his forehead and scanned the area, looking for the familiar low-slung shape of Sam's old sports car. It couldn't exactly be called one particular color, unless "rusty rainbow" fit the description. But right now it didn't matter as long as he got a ride. He couldn't wait to get home to check on his rain gauge and work some more on his anemometer.

SAM BENT TO TIE HIS SHOE for the third time. It was the only way he could think of to look inconspicuous in the hallway as the rest of the school cleared out. With all the rain outside, though, it looked like most people were taking a little longer—waiting for rides, standing at windows, maybe waiting for the latest downpour to ease up.

Problem was, this downpour just kept coming. And that could be just the ticket, if only he could get up the nerve.

He kept an eye on where she was standing with a cluster of her girlfriends, laughing and chatting. A couple of the girls wore colorful bright green cheerleading uniforms, and they peeled away first—probably to an after-school practice in the gym. That left Arielle Friesen (the prettiest girl in Bedford High) and two other girls.

Perfect.

He mentally rehearsed his line, which he'd been working on all afternoon but now had to deliver totally off the cuff, as if he'd made it up on the spot: Hey, does anybody need a ride home? I totally have room in my car.

Or maybe leave out the "totally," which sounded a little too California, unless maybe he should play up his San Diego roots, which could give him an edge. Or not.

Sam couldn't make up his mind. Either way, once he made his approach she would smile her beautiful smile at him, realize what a cool person he was, and say something like, "Hey, aren't you that cute guy in my biology class?"

Problem was, he couldn't think of a good way to temporarily ditch Christopher and Emily—unless he could talk them into taking the bus today instead of riding with him. Both of them were late.

He bent to tie his shoe one more time just as the bus rumbled past the windows outside.

Great. He kicked himself for not thinking ahead and for not telling them this morning that they would have to find another ride. Too late now.

"Sorry I'm late." Emily finally showed up, shuffling up behind him in the nearly empty hallway. "I had to get a book to read for English."

She held up a copy of *To Kill a Mockingbird* with a resigned look. Sam remembered reading that one in ninth grade too, and he couldn't help feeling bad for her.

"Sorry," he said. "Guess you'll live though."

Question was, would he? Sam glanced over his shoulder again toward the entry. Arielle had disappeared.

"What?" asked Emily.

"Oh, nothing." He hadn't meant to frown so obviously at the missed opportunity, as if he'd just bitten his tongue or stepped on a nail. "I was just wondering what happened to Christopher."

As if on cue, his younger brother appeared at the doors, smudging the plate-glass windows next to the entry doors and looking like a drowned lost puppy. After glancing up and down the halls a couple of times, his eyes finally brightened when he locked on them. He motioned for them to come outside.

"Coming," said Sam, though Christopher would not be able to hear him outside. Whatever. He and Emily headed for the door while he took one more look down the side hall, just in case Arielle had gone that way instead of outside.

But what could he do about it now anyway? He'd lost his chance. He figured she probably would never have accepted a ride from him, so maybe it didn't matter.

CHARLOTTE LOOKED OUT her kitchen window once again, checking to be sure the school bus made it safely, just in case the kids had had to abandon their little car. That wasn't such an outrageous idea, she told herself. Sam's car was so low to the ground, it wouldn't be able to handle much in the way of high waters. Not like a high-clearance four-wheel-drive truck.

What was Pete thinking when he gave that horrible, impractical little car to Sam? If the kids didn't make it home today, she would know whom to blame.

She held her breath as the school bus trundled by on its regular route, spraying runoff in both directions. It never even slowed down. Even Toby must have noticed from her dry spot on the porch; when Charlotte looked out to check, she noticed the dog wagging her tail furiously as the bus passed their driveway.

"Sorry, girl." Charlotte opened up the door and cracked open the screen. "But I'm sure they'll be home in a couple of minutes."

Or ten. Charlotte checked out the window at least that many times, watching for Sam's little car. She chided herself for worrying so much. It was just a little rain, and she'd been out driving in it herself just the day before. What was to worry about?

"Who-wee!" Pete blew in the way he always did, all bluster and noise. The shower followed him inside. "Did you hear the latest forecast?"

"Close that door!" she ordered. "And no, I didn't. But I'm guessing it's more rain."

"More rain is right. This weird system is just stalling

right over the top of us for some reason, and the wind is coming up—supposed to be gusts of up to forty. Guess I'll believe that when I see it. But it's been the rainiest April in twenty years, and if it keeps up they're talking serious flooding, and I don't think I want to be out there. Kids home from school yet?"

Charlotte checked out the window again, where ink-black clouds turned the afternoon sky to night.

"I take that as a no," said Pete, looking concerned as he joined her at the window. "Want me to go out and—"

"No, don't do that. They'll be here any minute. The bus just came by."

They stood quietly by the window for a moment until Pete snapped on the kitchen radio to hear the latest bad news. It was all that he'd said, and worse.

"Maybe they should have let school out early." Charlotte thought out loud.

"I don't know that they expected it to get this nasty," answered Pete.

"So where's your father?"

Pete nodded toward the barn. "Trying to get the generator fired up but not having much luck. Something in the fuel pump's not working, or else the carb's all gummed up, and—oh, hey. There they are."

He pointed toward the driveway at the little car bumping and splashing in their direction. At times it seemed to almost disappear into the puddles before it emerged again.

"In this kind of rain it looks more like a little submarine," said Pete, and Charlotte had to agree. But with the line of elm trees along the driveway bowing perilously low in the increasing gusts, and rain suddenly driving almost sideways, the good news was that they were home!

Or nearly home. When Charlotte opened the back door to step outside, a gust of wind wrested the doorknob from her hand and slammed it back around, out of her grasp.

"Mom!" Pete shouted and reached for the door, too late to stop its violent swing. And too late to stop the sickening sound of shattering glass, even over the howling wind.

Chapter Eight

Charlotte glanced over at the patched kitchen door as they ate their dinner that evening, late because of all the storm work Bob and Pete had needed to do. Among other things, Bob had attached a makeshift piece of plywood to cover the gaping hole where the glass window shattered. For now it did the job, even if it didn't earn any beauty points.

As they ate Christopher chattered even louder than the incessant rain pounding on the roof, and more than once Charlotte had to remind him not to feed Toby under the table, and to keep his attention on finishing the green beans on his plate, which were rapidly growing cold.

"You think this means they're going to cancel school tomorrow?" wondered Sam, sounding hopeful as he pushed the beans around on his plate too. Denise must not have taught them about finishing their veggies.

"You wish." Pete grinned at him and nodded toward the radio over on the counter. "If it does, we'll—"

The lights blinked just then, cutting him off in midsentence.

"Uh-oh." Now Sam dropped his fork and looked around. "What happens if we lose power?"

Christopher didn't miss the opportunity to tease his sister. "Then Emily won't be able to use her blow-dryer, is all."

But Emily didn't miss a beat either as she backhanded the comment. "We're not going to lose power. Grandpa has a generator, you know."

"Had." Pete looked over at his dad, and Bob didn't seem to be taking this conversation all that well as he frowned into his glass of milk.

"By the time we figured out what part we needed," he grumbled, sloshing his milk before taking another gulp, "AA was closed. I'll probably just run in tomorrow."

"Or not," answered Pete, "By tomorrow the roads may not be passable, if the forecasters are right. Heard 'em say it was going to be rainy for a few more days, at least. System's stalled here, and it just keeps dumping rain on us. It's the rainiest April in—"

"Look, Pete." Bob set the glass down a little too hard on the checkered tablecloth. "We can blame the forecasters or the nasty weather all we want. But when it comes right down to it, if you'd kept that thing serviced the way I told you to, we—"

"Dad, it's ancient, and you know it. Been sitting there for years, so if it's not one thing, it's the other. It wouldn't have made any difference if I'd been fussing with it or not, the generator's just a piece of—"

Charlotte gave him a warning look that fortunately curbed his tongue. Bob, on the other hand, wasn't backing down.

"Fact is, you keep things serviced, and it doesn't matter how old it gets. Good machinery is good machinery. Thought you knew that."

"I know we have a lot of that kind of stuff here at Heather Creek. But it's more like, old machinery is old machinery."

"All right, all right." Charlotte thought she'd best intervene before the finger-pointing got out of hand. If it wasn't the kids, it was the adults. "I don't think it does any good to blame each other, especially when neither of you can do anything about it. It's no one's fault. What's broken is broken, and it's just a piece of metal, after all."

"You got that part right," said Pete. "One big hunk of rusty metal."

"I don't know about any hunks," she told him, "but I'm sure we'll do just fine, no matter what happens."

"Even without a blow-dryer?" Christopher wasn't done teasing, but this time Emily ignored him. Instead, she returned to her salad and speared a carrot with her fork— but it squirted to the side and landed in Sam's lap.

"Hey, I don't want your carrots!" He scooted his chair from the table and threw it back at Emily, which could have escalated into a food fight if the lights hadn't blinked once more.

"We're going to wish we had that generator in a second or two." Bob wadded up his napkin and tossed it on the table just as the lights flickered and went out for good.

Christopher yelped in alarm, but Bob took charge.

"Stay where you are, kids," he told them. The lights remained off, and only the faintest shred of light filtered in from outside, barely enough to make out dark shapes. "I'll get a couple of flashlights. Charlotte, see if you can light some candles, or maybe those old lanterns of yours. Everybody else just stay put. No need to be tripping over each other. We've been through this before. You know what to do."

The way he said it, there was no question about doing anything else. Charlotte fumbled for the box of strike-anywhere matches in one of the cupboards by the sink and then located a couple of emergency candles on the top shelf. In less than a minute the candlelight cast a golden glow on their faces while shadows danced on the walls behind them.

"So now what?" Sam wondered out loud accenting his question with a whine. "No TV again, right? This is so lame. We never had power outages in San Diego. And now again . . ."

"It's just like in the ice storm," said Christopher, helping to light another candle. "But you don't need to worry about this one."

"Look who's telling us not to worry," said Sam. "You're the one who screamed like a girl the second the lights went out."

"Hey!" objected Emily. "*I* didn't scream."

"But Christopher did. That's all I'm saying . . ."

"Kwa-kwa-kwa." Count on Pete to make light of the situation, in a manner of speaking. As the kids continued their bickering he started making animal sounds while creating shadow-puppet shapes on the far wall and ceiling. One would think a thirty-something-year-old man would know better, but at least it finally caught the kids' attention, and the arguing subsided for a time.

"How did you do that?" Christopher wanted to know as he clasped his own fingers together, trying to mimic what his uncle had done. The result looked more like a lopsided turkey, but they all laughed nonetheless.

"Here, let me try." Now Sam got into the act, and before long the ceiling was filled with a menagerie of wolves, geese, elves, trolls, and dragons of every sort. A battle rapidly ensued, and Sam's wolf soon ate Pete's dragon, which brought another laugh from everyone—even Bob.

"Come on, Grandpa," said Christopher. "Let's see what you can make!"

"I should get outside." Bob hesitated, and Charlotte knew he might have refused. But then he looked down at his big, rough farmer's hands and knit them together, as if he was getting ready to pray. The funniest thing wasn't the exquisite swan he flew across the ceiling of the kitchen, its shadow lengthening from one wall to the next. The funniest thing was the squawking sound he made, deep in his throat, and very much like a distant bird migrating past the farm this spring. Even Toby looked up at him from her spot in the corner of the room and cocked her head sideways.

"See, the coolest ones only come out when the power goes down," Pete explained, hiding a smile but not very well. "Last time I saw that bird I was sitting around a campfire on a Boy Scout campout at Crystal Lake when I was twelve. The scoutmaster actually talked Dad into coming along."

"Talked me into coming?" Bob promptly unfolded his

hands, the moment gone just as a swan might have been frightened from its nest. "Maybe you don't remember that long ago, but I volunteered, young man."

"All I remember was when Jeff Simons wandered off in the middle of the night, and you had to go pull him out of the marsh, and he was like covered with mud. Looked like a chocolate-covered Boy Scout, remember?"

"I remember he shouldn't have been out by himself that time of night."

"And you sure laid that lecture on him before you sent him home." Pete wagged a finger in his best angry-father imitation. "Made me real glad it wasn't me."

A smile passed between father and son, but only for a moment, and then it flickered away in the shadows. By that time, however, Charlotte had an idea. Before anyone could escape the dinner table or slip away to their room, she had returned with a box in hand.

"Okay, everybody sit down except Pete, who's going to clear the table." She pointed at the dishes. "Just over there on the kitchen counter will be fine, Pete."

"Aye, aye." He saluted before scooping up several plates. "But I have dibs on the race car."

"You have dibs on absolutely nothing. We're going to let the kids choose their game pieces, starting with Emily." She pulled back the lid to their worn Monopoly game and extended it to her granddaughter. "Emily, you choose your favorite."

Emily paused for a moment, wrinkling her nose.

"You've played before, haven't you?" Charlotte couldn't imagine anyone not having played Monopoly. But Emily just shrugged.

"I don't think anybody in San Diego plays it."

"Not if it doesn't have batteries," added Sam.

"Oh, come on." Pete cleared off the rest of the plates. "We used to play this all the time when I was a kid. It's the only game Mom can beat me at, but that's 'cause she cheats."

"Pete!" Charlotte objected. "That is absolutely not true."

Pete ignored the objection.

"Anyway, Emily," he went on, "you guys could even play it at your birthday party this weekend. Like have an all-night Monopoly tournament. What do you think?"

"I get the cannon!" At least Christopher knew what he wanted, and Sam snapped up the race car while Bob was stuck with the boot and Charlotte took the thimble. But at the mention of her birthday, Emily only frowned, looking out the window.

"I think if this keeps up," she mumbled, "there won't be a birthday party."

"Trust me." Pete took out the little dog playing piece and plunked it down in front of Emily. "The power's probably going to come back on in just a few minutes. Or maybe it's just here, like a tree fell on our line or something. And even if it doesn't come back on tonight, we're going to have your party if we have to hold it on Noah's ark. Right, Mom?"

Emily didn't appear quite convinced, but she did pick up the little pewter dog to examine it carefully, and Charlotte thought she saw her granddaughter's expression thaw just a little.

"It's kind of cute," Emily finally admitted. "So how do we play?"

Between Charlotte and Pete, they explained the basic rules while Pete served as banker and distributed the play money. Emily set up her bills methodically on the tabletop in front of her while Christopher and Sam piled theirs in one stack apiece. Bob kept glancing out the window, though by now the only thing they could see was the glitter of raindrops cascading down windowpanes.

"Your turn, Grandpa." Charlotte nudged him to take the dice for his first roll. "Whatever's out there will still be out there when the power returns."

"I really ought to be checking on the animals," he told her as the wind gusted once again, rattling every window in the house. "Sounds like the barn's about to blow over. The horses are probably nervous out there in that weather."

Well, he could be right about that, but Charlotte figured that was the last thing the kids needed to hear. She gulped and tried not to telegraph her worry as she rested a hand on his shoulder to keep him from bolting.

"Everything's going to be just fine," she told him, as much for Emily, Sam, and Christopher to hear as for anything else. The phone rang just then, and everyone at the table jumped.

"I thought the power was out!" said Christopher.

"Power, yes," replied Pete, rearranging his stacks of play money in front of him. "Phone, no."

That would apply to the old-fashioned wall phone, Charlotte knew, and just then she was grateful Bob had refused to buy a cordless model the last time they were shopping at the warehouse store in Harding. Since she was sitting closest to the phone, she reached over and grabbed the receiver off the hook.

"Mom?" Her son Bill sounded farther away than just two towns over. "Are you guys okay over there? We've been hearing reports of flooding your way."

"Snug as a bug in a rug," she replied, forcing her voice to sound several shades more chipper than she felt. "We're all here around the kitchen table, enjoying a game of Monopoly by candlelight."

"Oh. So your power's out?" Surely he didn't sound disappointed? "You know the creek's about to flood, don't you?"

"Oh, I'm sure it'll be fine, Bill. How are Anna and the kids?"

"Fine, fine. Don't forget we're a little higher upstream here in River Bend than you are there at the farm. Though, come to think of it, the Carters and some of the others down on that end of the creek will be the first to flood, right? Heard from any of them?"

"That's nice of you to ask, but no, not yet. Maybe I'll give Hannah a call."

She imagined what it would take to submerge neighboring fields under these floodwaters. Not much, really. Especially at the low-lying Carter place. But in the past most of the major floods had come about as a result of untimely spring thaws, or a combination of thaw and rain, or ice backing up drainage pipes. Not incessant rain, like now.

"Well, you call me if it gets worse," he told her. "It's raining buckets here."

"Yes, will do. Take care now—" Suddenly all Charlotte heard was silence.

"Line went dead," Charlotte reported, her voice flat.

Pete's forehead furrowed as he looked out the window.

"I think we're losing trees out there now," he told them. "Maybe the storm's taking out more than we thought. The weather report really didn't say anything about this, you know."

As if on cue, they heard a sharp crack above the thundering noise of the wind and rain. Even if they couldn't see what was going on outside, clearly Pete was right about the trees. They all looked at each other with wide eyes until Bob picked up the little leather cup and began shaking dice. Charlotte was just grateful he hadn't pulled on his boots and rushed out to try to fix things. By this time he really couldn't do much anyway, and heaven knew she didn't want him slogging around out in the dark and rain, getting himself hurt.

"Okay," he said, his jaw working and the muscles in his neck tensed up like violin strings. "Like you said, nothing we can do about it. My turn, right?"

Chapter Nine

The next morning Charlotte caught Bob staring out the kitchen window at the soggy mess between their house and barn, his arms crossed and his jaw set—the same as he'd been the night before. Broken tree branches littered the parking area while two of the closer trees lining the driveway had fallen entirely. Who knew what else had happened in the night?

"Wind's eased up for now," he reported. "Phone and power still out. Rain's still coming. That system . . ."

"Yes, we know all about that system." She pulled her terry cloth robe a little closer as she came up behind him. So there was no use trying the kitchen light or the phone. "Looks like you and Pete are going to have some cleanup to do today."

"We'll need a little help," he replied, nodding toward the battery-powered radio. "Word is, school's canceled for the day because of flooding, so the kids aren't going anyplace soon."

He must have been up early, listening to the radio. Strange that she hadn't heard him.

"The roads? Did they say anything about the roads?"

"Standing water's keeping buses from running."

"Which means Heather Creek—"

"Has already busted over its banks, and there's still more rain to come. Phone and power lines are out all over the place, but they're working on them."

This could not be good. Charlotte cleared the Monopoly game box off the kitchen table and went to fix them some coffee, before she remembered the coffeemaker wouldn't work without power. Neither would the overhead light, or the refrigerator—at least not until Bob got the generator running. If he could.

She also knew she shouldn't turn on the water, as the remaining pressure from their well's storage tank would quickly dissipate without power to bring it back up. And then what?

A little water would be okay though. She would just have to heat it on the corn-burning stove in the living room, the old-fashioned way, the way her father used to at their house when she was a girl and family came on Sunday afternoons for pie and coffee. Thankfully Bob had already fired up the cast-iron parlor stove, where a small fire crackled cheerfully. All that, and she still hadn't heard him?

"I must have been sleeping hard," she said, "to not have heard you get up."

"Didn't make much noise. Not like the rain all night."

Come to think of it, she had awakened several times to the unusually loud sound of rain pounding on their roof and windows.

"Let me at least make you some coffee," she told him, "before you go out there."

He nodded and kept his arms crossed and his gaze fixed on the never-ending storm. She wouldn't have minded so much if the sun had made a brief appearance this morning. But even if the driving wind had let up for now, the clouds overhead looked as dark and foreboding as ever. She shivered and mixed up a quick batch of camp coffee, straining the grounds from the brew with a sieve. Bob probably wouldn't be able to tell the difference, as long as it was hot.

"When do they say it's going to clear?" she wondered out loud a few minutes later. Bob would have heard that too.

"They didn't."

In Bob's abbreviated man-speak, that could have meant the weather announcer hadn't yet said when it was expected to clear. Or it could have meant the announcer had specifically said there was no sign of the weather clearing in the near future. One more glance out the window told her it was probably the latter.

Either way, Bob accepted the steaming mug with one hand and shrugged on a rain slicker with the other. Then he headed for the door.

"Send 'em out soon as they wake up," he told her, "but no later than seven."

By the clock on the kitchen wall that meant the kids had just ten more minutes to sleep. On the other hand, Christopher's radio alarm had battery backup and should have been sounding by now, blaring out a few bars from a popular rock tune. Charlotte didn't much care for the morning serenade, but it did the job.

Sam came sleepwalking down the stairs a few minutes

later, still in a worn pair of sweatpants and a wrinkled T-shirt and scratching his wild head of curly dark hair, mumbling something about Christopher's dumb alarm. He barely looked at his grandmother as he plopped down at the table, set his cell phone aside, and reached for a box of cornflakes.

"Don't get too comfortable," she told him, trying to keep her voice soft. "There's no school today, but Grandpa's going to need your help clearing things away."

"Uh-huh." Sam appeared not to have heard or understood, just poured his cereal and nibbled on a few flakes as he checked his phone. Which gave Charlotte an idea.

"Why didn't I think of it last night?" she said, leaning closer and reaching for the phone. "May I?"

"Huh?" Finally Sam started to wake, but he didn't seem to understand Charlotte's intent. How could he?

"Will it work for me to call Hannah with this thing?" She held the little black phone gingerly, studying the little symbols and wondering how real fingers could work such tiny keys.

"Yeah, but you know we have such lousy coverage out here. See?" He pointed at a couple of the symbols, including one that looked like a pair of tiny grain elevators. "Only two bars. No, one. Sometimes there aren't even that many."

"Bars are good, as I recall."

"Bars are good. Just punch in the number you want, Grandma. Battery's almost dead again, but you can try."

She carefully keyed in Hannah's home number, and then pressed the phone to her ear and waited. Sam reached over and took it from her.

"You've got to press the CALL button, Grandma."

"Oh, of course. Now I remember."

She waited again, and this time only heard an unpleasant tone and a mechanical operator's voice apologizing that the number she had dialed had been disconnected or was out of service and saying she should please try again later.

"That can't be right," Charlotte handed the phone back. "Disconnected?"

"Their line must be down too. See, but if everybody had cell phones, you wouldn't have this problem. And if she *has* a cell phone, you need to know the number."

"Oh yes!" She hurried to the notepad by the kitchen phone and searched for Hannah's cell phone number. Why hadn't she thought of that before?

But a moment later Charlotte sighed again at the sound of Hannah's recorded voice asking her to leave a message, and saying she'd return the call as soon as possible.

"Hannah, it's me. I'm calling on Sam's phone since it looks like our regular phone lines are down. Call me as soon as you can at . . ." She looked to Sam for the number, but he only shook his head and tried to tell her something she didn't understand. So she covered the receiver with her hand.

"She'll get it," Sam repeated. "It's on her caller ID."

"Oh." Charlotte wasn't quite sure what that meant, but she added the information to her message and hung up. And for the first time she wondered if it might not be a good idea to look into getting one of these little cell phones for herself. If only the buttons were a little larger and the screen didn't have so many tiny symbols.

"Woo-HOO!" Christopher yelped as he bounded down

the stairs. No problem waking *him* up. "Did you hear, Sam? It was on the radio. No school today! We can play all day!"

Charlotte corralled her youngest grandson when he had made it down the stairs, sitting him down at the table and bringing him a pitcher of milk. She closed the refrigerator door as quickly as she could to keep in the cold.

"Don't look now." Sam shoveled another bite of flakes into his mouth without looking up. "But we have to help Grandpa and Uncle Pete."

Christopher looked as if he didn't believe it, pointing to the rain-soaked barnyard. By now the faint sound of a chainsaw rumbled above the constant downpour, from where Pete was clearing away debris.

"Out there? You're joking."

"Wish I was."

By that time, however, Charlotte had retreated to her bedroom to change. She found her oldest pair of jeans in a bottom drawer, along with a frayed, blue-speckled long-sleeve sweatshirt she'd used when they'd painted the kitchen last year. Rubber boots by the back door and an oversized rain poncho completed her outfit.

"I think Uncle Pete is out there cutting up fallen trees." She pointed in the direction of the driveway. "I'm going to go with your grandfather to see how the Carters are doing."

"The Carters—" began Sam.

"I want you to stay here and do what your Uncle Pete tells you. No video games. All right?"

Oh, I forgot. Charlotte realized what she'd just said but didn't correct herself. No power, either.

"But wait!" Christopher called after her as she opened

the back door. "How are you going to get to the Carters' place?"

Too late. She had already stepped out into the rain, closing the door behind her. Good thing the wind had abated, for the most part. But she was greeted by a sheet of rain, which pummeled her poncho and sought out every seam and hole in its hood. Before she knew it, rain was running down her neck.

"Bob?" she called, but the rain swallowed her feeble voice, so she put her head down and hurried for the barn. Of course the rain didn't stop Toby from following.

A few minutes of searching brought her around to the back of the barn, where Bob knelt next to their generator, only partly sheltered by a lean-to he'd constructed for the machinery. He paused with the wrench in midair when he saw her.

"What are you doing out here? Where are the kids?"

"I need you to take me to see if Hannah is all right. We tried on Sam's cell phone, but we still couldn't get through."

He picked up his wrench and fiddled with his generator, not answering.

"I'm serious, Bob. They could be flooded out, or worse."

He sighed. "Look, Charlotte. If I don't get this generator going, we don't have water, despite what you see all around you. We can't drink out of mud puddles, you know."

"You said you didn't have the right part."

"Well, I'm trying something else."

"Is it going to work?"

He paused for a moment, and then sighed again and dropped his wrench.

"No."

"Then why don't you see if the Carters might have the part you need? Doesn't Frank have a generator too?"

He seemed to consider her idea for a moment before scratching his muddy cheek and nodding. She helped him to his feet and trudged through ankle-deep mud with him to the barn, where his newest John Deere was stored.

Of course, by "newest," that still meant a twenty-five-year-old tractor. They'd purchased it new from AA Tractor when Pete was still . . . what, about ten? But by the gleam in its green paint, one would never have guessed its age, and it roared to life the moment Bob pushed the starter. He pointed for her to sit in the black bucket seat while he perched in front of her.

"You sure you can drive like this?" she asked, climbing to her place.

"Hang on."

Bob maneuvered the tractor into gear, powering up as they headed out into the storm and down the drive. Chainsaw in hand, Pete didn't hear them until they had steered around the fallen elm he'd been sawing into pieces. He paused and looked up at them while Bob slowed and Charlotte cupped her hands around her mouth to shout.

"We're going to go check on the Carters," she yelled, but Pete didn't quite follow. He held a hand to his ear.

"The CARTERS!" boomed her husband as he gunned the engine so that they jerked ahead through the mud and rain. "Keep the dog here."

The tractor's enormous back wheels should have no trouble negotiating puddles, ponds, or just about anything that lay between Heather Creek Farm and the Carters' place, perhaps a mile downstream. Well, at least Charlotte hoped not.

But since Hannah and Frank's place was situated on a lovely but low-lying meadow bordering a deep spot in the creek, she feared that any flooding might directly affect them before anyone else. Still she prayed quietly as they chugged along the deserted highway, and as muddy floodwaters lapped up against the tractor so high she lifted her feet and was afraid to look down.

"Lord," she whispered, clenching her teeth and gripping the seat with both hands, "please keep Hannah and Frank safe. Keep us all safe."

Chapter Ten

I was afraid of that.

Charlotte squinted through the rain as Bob eased off the throttle of their tractor and the Carter farm finally came into view. Bob just pressed his lips together, saying nothing, but that was enough.

Any other time, she could think of no more idyllic setting than Carter's Hollow, as the kids liked to call it. Frank took unusual pride in maintaining his park-like setting, with well-watered golf-course grass that sloped gently down to the banks of Heather Creek, where it was lined with cottonwoods shading a picnic spot with two tables, a swing, and a fire ring.

But in recent years the Carters had had more than their share of bad luck. A neatly stacked pile of firewood was all that was left of the tree that had crashed into their porch during a winter storm not too long ago. Frank had already patched and repaired all the damage—everything except painting the new trim to match.

Now the usually placid creek had turned against them, viciously washing over the benches attached to the picnic tables and nearly ripping off the seat of the swing.

And that wasn't the worst of it. Although Frank and Hannah's home was situated nearly a hundred yards back from the usual banks of the creek on a rise several yards high, the creek's muddy rising waters had quickly made up the difference and now lapped halfway across the once-manicured lawn. Much higher, and the Carter home would be turned into an island, or worse.

No time to worry about all that. Once more Bob gunned the engine as they jerked ahead toward the disaster, where Frank and Hannah were struggling to unload a large sack from the back of their truck into the side yard. Frank had parked by the front steps of the house, out of reach of the ascending floodwaters for the moment. Although they had apparently already dumped a pile of sandbags on the lawn, it hardly looked like enough to make a difference.

"Frank!" Bob yelled, and the Carters paused to look up. Neither wore raingear; both looked soaked to the skin and up to their ankles in mud.

Frank had very little hair these days, but Hannah's short, graying-blonde hair was plastered to her head, adding to her tragic look. Her favorite pink sweatshirt with the goose on the front looked soiled and muddy too.

Poor girl, thought Charlotte, a lump rising in her throat —until she realized that she probably didn't look much better.

Hannah's face lit up when she recognized who had come to help. Bob cut the tractor's engine as they rolled to a soggy stop next to the truck. Tall and slim like his wife, Frank teetered under the weight of the sandbag before letting it drop to their feet.

"Nice day, huh?" Frank had a way with understatement. He and Bob shook hands as if they were meeting at the feed store on a sunny day. "Good of you to stop by."

"We had no idea," Charlotte told Hannah, returning her friend's grateful hug. "I wish you could have called us earlier."

"Actually we tried," answered Hannah. Her face looked drawn and pale, with very little of its usual sunshine. "But our phones went out. I don't know about yours."

Charlotte kept a protective arm around her friend.

"Ours, too. Dear friend, I'm so sorry we didn't get here before this. We even tried with Sam's cell phone."

"The cell phone!" Hannah brought a hand to her cheek. "That's what that thing is for, isn't it? I'm so silly. I haven't even had it turned on!"

Charlotte smiled. "It doesn't matter now. We just didn't know it would keep coming down like this. The weather reports didn't tell us how bad it was going to be."

"You couldn't have known, and besides, you couldn't have come in all the wind." Hannah shook her head as she looked around. "At least we didn't lose any more trees. But we almost didn't make it back from town this morning."

"Don't tell me you were out on the roads?" Charlotte couldn't believe it, not after what they'd seen.

"See that mark?" Frank almost looked proud as he tapped the side of his truck with the toe of his boot. A muddy line gave witness to how the floodwaters had nearly risen over the floorboards. "Hannah was getting a little nervous, I think."

"A little?" Hannah corrected him. "I thought we were going to die."

"Well." Frank took up another end of a sandbag with big hands. "If it helps, I wouldn't advise anybody else taking the route we did. Water's likely a half-foot higher by now."

Still the rain poured all around them, and for a quiet moment Charlotte tried not to think how close her friend might have come to disaster this morning. Finally Bob straightened up.

"Well, we didn't come to chat." He grabbed the other side of the nearest sandbag in the back of the truck. "But I tell you, if I'd known things was getting this bad, I would have brought some sandbags of my own."

Charlotte looked at the pile of sandbags on the lawn and the pile of sand remaining in the back of the truck, and she knew he was right. These were not going to go very far.

"What else can we do?" She would need to keep a hopeful expression despite the water creeping up the lawn. Frank bit his lip, wiped the back of his hand across his face, and nodded toward the battle line.

"All right, how about you girls get shovels and help us fill the bags we got. Bob and I will start building a wall on the creek side of the house."

He grunted as he grabbed a filled bag by its two upper corners, and then waddled across the lawn toward the rising water. "So whose bright idea was it to build this close to the creek anyway?" he mumbled.

Charlotte wasn't sure which pioneer had fancied this

spot but guessed the decision had been made several generations earlier, probably on a warm summer day under a calm blue sky. Right now they were as far away from that scene as anyone could imagine. She crawled up into the back of the truck and turned to give Hannah a hand. They would shovel what sand they had and then decide what to do from there. Hannah gamely grabbed a shovel and dug in.

In a moment they formed an assembly line of sorts, with Charlotte and Hannah alternately shoveling wet sand from the truck into waiting sacks held by Bob and Frank. A rush of adrenaline and the realization that Hannah's home was in real danger kept Charlotte going at first, but after a few bags she worried that she would not be able to keep up. A shovelful missed its mark.

"I'm sorry," she told Bob, but maybe he didn't hear her over the growing roar of the stream and the constant downpour. By that time her arms had begun to ache, and her hands were shaking with the effort. She felt a blister forming on the palm of one hand. Perhaps Hannah felt the same way.

"Are you all right?" asked Hannah.

Charlotte nodded quickly, though she could not be sure of herself. This kind of shoveling was entirely different than puttering about the garden on a fine spring day when she could pause to rest or go inside for a glass of lemonade.

She did pause for breath, though she feared if she paused too long she might not be able to make her arms move again. The sound of rushing water seemed to grow louder still, along with the distant sound of thunder—or perhaps it was a tractor.

There would be nothing unusual about that, except on a day like today. The tractor noise grew louder though, and it made her wonder.

Who would be crazy enough to be out in the fields *now*? They could get bogged down in the mud, and there would be no way to pull them free.

But the distinct chugging and wheezing of an older machine grew louder and louder, enough so that she paused to look around. Coming down the road—there! She spotted their own ancient tractor, with someone who looked an awful lot like Pete at the wheel. The tractor was pulling a large open utility trailer piled high with sand.

And three more figures were riding the rails of the trailer! One of them, the smallest, straightened and waved wildly.

"To the rescue!" Christopher yelled, waving as they neared the Carter farm and Hannah scraped the last of the sand from their truck bed. "We've come to the rescue!"

Perfect timing, as a matter of fact. Pete pulled up, jockeying the controls. "We had this for some building projects," he told them, never taking his eyes off the rising floodwaters, "and I got to thinking you guys might need it more than we do. 'Cause if anybody's going to flood, it's going to be—"

"I was hoping you'd come," Bob interrupted, returning from another run. He flashed the hint of a grin at his son. "Actually, if you could nudge it down a little closer to the water, we'll be able to place 'em that much faster. Creek's still rising."

Pete started up the tractor again with a nod. "You got it. I just don't want to sink the rig in this mud."

"Yeah, well if we don't pick up the pace, we're going to lose the house anyway, so maybe it doesn't matter."

Pete nodded and made for the water's edge right after the three kids hopped off and stood in the rain, looking quite unsure of what to do next. Bob took care of that in a hurry.

"Emily and Christopher, get two more shovels," he barked. "Frank can show you if you don't know where to find them. Sam, you grab the bags and place them with me."

The kids did as they were told, shoveling and piling and scurrying between the tractors and the creek. Within a few minutes they'd laid a foundation of sandbags in a semicircle around the lower side of the house, quickly adding to it a second layer.

"Starting to look like something," observed Sam, and Charlotte nodded. Although the water hadn't quite reached the bags yet, she could tell—or she prayed—that their efforts might hold back some of the flood.

"Good job," she told him. "Just a few more."

That would be all the sand they had left, with precious few bags to spare.

Sam grabbed a filled bag before his grandfather returned from the river, but it was obvious by this time that he would not be able to carry it solo. He faltered like a tree in a storm until Charlotte jumped down to give him a hand.

"I've got it," he told her, though he most obviously did not. But as soon as Charlotte wrestled the other end of the sack from his grip, a spasm of pain in her lower back nearly doubled her over, as if a violin string had been plucked and snapped. She gasped and fell to her knees, dropping the bag and clutching her back.

"Ohh!" she moaned. She hadn't felt this kind of intense pain in years—perhaps not since Pete was born. She could not move, or breathe, or even speak. Hannah flew to her side in an instant.

"Charlotte? What can I do to help you?"

Charlotte couldn't answer.

"Oh, man! I'm sorry, Grandma." Sam looked down at her with concern written all over his face. "I shouldn't have let you do that. It's my fault."

She shook her head and tried to breathe quick, shallow breaths.

"Not . . . your . . . fault," she whispered as Hannah helped her maneuver to lean against the truck. But no matter whose fault it was, everything hurt like blazes, and this was definitely the wrong time for her to throw out her back.

"Here, I'll go get Bob to help you back inside," Hannah decided. "He can—"

"No!" Charlotte gripped her friend's arm so tightly she was afraid she might have dug in her fingernails. "They're too busy for something like this."

True enough, Bob and Frank apparently hadn't yet noticed Charlotte's problems as they piled the last row of sandbags.

"Are you sure?" Hannah looked toward the river uncertainly, and Charlotte nodded.

"Just get me up to the porch for a second; let me catch my breath. I'll be okay in just a couple of minutes."

Or so she hoped.

Hannah did as she was asked, lending Charlotte her shoulder so she could hobble with painful difficulty up the back steps and into the house.

"Don't you tell Bob!" Charlotte warned her, mincing her steps through the mudroom and kitchen. Hannah helped her remove her muddy boots, one at a time.

"Charlotte," she said, setting aside the boots. "Don't you think—"

"Not a word!"

Chapter
Eleven

From then on, Charlotte wasn't much help to the sandbagging efforts at the Carter farm, no matter how much she would have liked to do something. She couldn't do anything except lie in pain on Hannah's parlor sofa while Hannah brought her some pain relievers.

"Really, Hannah. I should be feeling just fine here in a moment." Charlotte wasn't sure how much her optimism could influence her recovery time, but thought it worth a try. But when she tried to sit up, tears came to her eyes.

"Charlotte!" cried Hannah. "What are you doing? Lie down if it hurts so much. Please!"

"I've felt worse," Charlotte managed through clenched teeth. She mopped her face with a tissue. "Although I have to admit something like this makes me feel awfully old and decrepit."

"Nothing to do with age." Hannah tried to correct her. "You know my nephew has terrible back problems, and he's only in his early twenties."

"And what does he do about it?"

"Well, ah . . ." Hannah turned away without answering, looked back toward the kitchen, and pointed out the back window. "Have you seen? Three rows of sandbags! I feel much better now."

"So do I." Charlotte struggled to her feet, trying unsuccessfully not to bend her aching back. She caught her breath at the nasty twinges of pain, and then hobbled in lockstep across the linoleum to see for herself.

"Charlotte! You really can't be doing this." Hannah gently took her by the shoulders and tried to guide her back to the sofa, but Charlotte refused.

"I can, and I will. Now, thanks for the nursing care, honey, but I'll be fine from here. There's just too much to do right now to be an invalid on your sofa."

Hannah frowned and shook her head but didn't try to stop Charlotte from hobbling back outside to the covered back porch. From there they could both see how the sandbag soldiers were doing. Maybe Hannah was right: it would take quite the floodwaters to breach this barrier.

The kids must have agreed, because by this time Christopher had climbed to the top of the knee-high wall, balancing precariously. He turned and waved his hands menacingly.

"Nyah-nyah," he told the waters loudly enough for all to hear. "Now try and come up here."

"Christopher!" His uncle stepped over and scooped the boy up under his arm, lifting him up and setting him down on the uphill side. "You're going to knock our wall down. It's not to play on."

Despite Pete's tone, the other kids laughed; the momentary relief in the midst of all the mud and rain probably did them all good. Still, Charlotte couldn't help shivering as the rain continued to pelt them without letup and the waters continued to creep upward. She hoped the wall would not be tested, but right now it seemed inevitable.

"I can't tell you what this means to me. No way could we have done this alone." Hannah slipped her arm around Charlotte's waist, and Charlotte had to bite her tongue not to cry out in pain.

"That's what we're here for."

Behind them, the sudden ring of a telephone made Charlotte jump.

"Goodness!" Hannah turned and ran back inside. "The phones must be back up!"

A few moments later Charlotte looked back through the screen door to see Hannah holding her kitchen phone to one ear and nodding seriously.

"All right," she said, and the dead-serious expression on her face told Charlotte it was not good news. "I understand."

As she spoke, she stretched the olive-green phone cord to its full length, and then cupped a hand over the receiver to holler through the screen.

"It's Eulalia Barry, Frank. They've got water right up to their back steps, and it's rising fast."

"The phone's working again?" he wondered out loud.

"Of course the phone's working again." Her voice strained above the sound of the rain, but just barely. "What do I tell them?"

"We'll need to get some more sand," he answered, running a hand over his wet head. By this time everyone else stood at attention behind him. "Tell them to hold on, and we'll be there in ten minutes."

They sprang into action again, grabbing the unused sandbags and throwing shovels into the trailer. Pete fired up his tractor once more, and Bob did the same. Charlotte fought back tears as she climbed into the trailer with her grandchildren. She wasn't quite sure what she could do now, in her condition; she just knew she had to be there with the kids.

"You okay, Grandma?" wondered Sam.

She flashed a wan smile and nodded as vigorously as she dared.

"Of course I'm okay. You think I'm an old lady, do you?"

She didn't want to hear the answer. Meanwhile, Frank pointed back at Hannah in the doorway, still clutching the revived telephone.

"Call Jake at the quarry," he told her. "Tell him to meet us at the Barry place with a load of sand as soon as he can."

"But the roads—"

"Hang the roads. If we don't get sand, people are going to . . . well, just tell him!"

"What if he doesn't answer the phone?"

"Then call 9-1-1."

With that, their unlikely rescue caravan of three tractors pulled away, first down the Carters' gravel driveway and then parallel to the creek toward several more threatened homes. Around them, the fields had already flooded, but they skirted the worst of the flooding on their way to the Barry farm, on the other side of the Stevenson property.

Charlotte gripped the railing of the open trailer, dreading every bump and biting her lip to keep from crying out. Sam eyed her warily, but she turned her most pleasant expression on him.

"Nothing a farm girl can't handle," she told him, wishing it were true. Christopher and Emily didn't seem to notice the exchange as they huddled under their rain hoods, apparently lost in their own thoughts.

It had been too long since breakfast, and the rush of adrenaline that had kept them working for several hours at the Carter farm now drained from Charlotte more completely than she'd imagined. It was all she could do not to collapse into the wet, gritty bed of the trailer.

"This is kind of cool," Christopher said without warning. *Cool* was not the word she would have used, unless it referred to the cold rain that now made her shiver. But of course Christopher had another take on things. "We're the rescue squad."

"That we are." Charlotte took his lead, as much to help keep up morale among them as to take her mind off the pain. Bob looked back at them, but not because he could hear what they said—surely he couldn't. Instead, his glance told her that he recognized she was not all right. She smiled back in his direction, knowing full well she wasn't fooling him for a moment.

"Are we almost there?" asked Emily. She had worked well and without complaint with Sam for the past several hours.

"Just ahead, dear." Charlotte clenched her teeth and fought off spasms of pain as they plowed through the muddy lanes that had turned to rivers and were closing in on the Barry farm.

Eulalia and Dick Barry operated one of the more modest farms in the county. Their older, white, one-story frame house was shaded by two ancient oaks at the front corners;

there was a small barn out back and a toolshed on the other side of the drive. In appearance it had little in common with the Carter place, except that it had frontage on Heather Creek and also had been built a little too close to the watershed. Usually hidden behind a thick row of cottonwoods along the back of the property, the creek's waters had unabashedly burst through to see if they could claim a victim. Old Mr. Barry met them with an antique dining room chair in hand as he stepped out his front door.

"You're just in time to help me move some stuff out to the barn," he told them, motioning back over his shoulder. The stooped older man hardly stood taller than Christopher. "Up in the loft, where the water won't get to it."

"You do what you have to do," Bob told him. "We're going to set some sandbags around the back of your house."

That suited Mr. Barry just fine, but while they waited for Jake to arrive with his load of sand, Charlotte looked in on Mrs. Barry to see how she was doing.

"In fifty years, I've never seen it like this," said the tiny gray-haired woman as she scurried from her back window to the front door and back again. Charlotte didn't try to keep up with her. She just waited until Mrs. Barry returned to the kitchen. Overhead the rain pounded on the roof, making conversation a challenge.

"And if this keeps up," Mrs. Barry went on, "we're going to be under water in a few minutes."

"No, Mrs. Barry." Charlotte did her best to stay optimistic. "I'm sure the men will—"

"But I'm not going to leave, you know. We're staying."

Lacking a second floor, the rattled Mrs. Barry had already piled pots and pans from her lower cupboards onto the counter, along with chairs, two pink wastebaskets, a glass vase containing plastic gardenias, and an exceptionally high pile of vintage Betty Crocker cookbooks stuffed with yellowed news clippings and recipes. Over the next several minutes she moved a framed picture of Jesus from one counter to the other, placing it carefully next to the books. Then she grabbed an old-fashioned vacuum cleaner and started to work on a small circular rug by the back door.

"Here, Mrs. Barry, look." Charlotte came up beside her and eased the sweeper from the woman's gnarled, arthritic hands. "The men are going to do their best to keep the flood from coming this far. See? They're setting up sandbags right now."

Sure enough, a beeping sound told her Jake's dump truck had finally made it through, and they watched through the little kitchen window as he left a load of sand in ankle-deep floodwaters just outside the door. If they had waited much longer, there might not have been much point.

Still Mrs. Barry could not be comforted as she fretted over low-hanging drapes and moved boxes of dishes from one table to another. Charlotte finally gave up trying to help and instead stood watching through the back window.

"We're not going to leave," repeated Mrs. Barry.

"You may not have to." Charlotte kept her arms folded across her chest, trying not to move. Her back felt a little better that way, or maybe the pain pills were finally kicking in.

Charlotte couldn't remember ever having been inside

the little house—though she thought perhaps Hannah had visited on several occasions. Come to think of it, hadn't Hannah mentioned a cat?

"Er, Mrs. Barry." She turned to see the old woman on her knees by the refrigerator, sweeping out dust bunnies with a hand broom. "Did you have an animal in here with you?"

Mrs. Barry's cat answered the question for himself, and Charlotte followed the soft yowl up to a cardboard box perched precariously on top of the harvest-gold appliance. A black paw emerged from a small round breathing hole, clawing at the air before disappearing once again.

"Do you think Risky will be all right up there?" asked Mrs. Barry, her question sincere. Charlotte helped the woman to her feet, ignoring the twinge in her own back.

"I'm sure he'll be fine, Mrs. Barry."

"Because I wouldn't want him to be scared." Tears filled Mrs. Barry's eyes as they watched the sandbags go up around the back of the house, and as more and more tractors and trucks arrived over the next little while. There was Dan Hostetler and Hank Richmond. Dave and DeeDee Myers. The Andreasson brothers, back from college. Hank whistled and gestured as a backhoe jockeyed into position and lowered several bags into place at once.

For a moment Charlotte thought she should have been out there in the rain with them, working to save the farm. But now, as she stood in Mrs. Barry's kitchen, her arm around the frail old woman, she knew she was in the right place.

"Are those your grandchildren?" asked Mrs. Barry, finally still enough to notice. Christopher turned around just then from shoveling sand into bags and gave them a thumbs-up.

"That's my younger grandson there."

"He looks like a good little worker. And your grand-daughter? The pretty one? How old is she?"

"Fourteen. Actually—" Charlotte caught herself. "Turning fifteen in . . . goodness, just three days from now. I haven't had time to think about it, with all this weather trouble."

"Well, I think we need to fix them all some lunch."

As Mrs. Barry moved back to her kitchen Christopher turned his attention to something else out of their view, around the side of the house. Charlotte thought she heard shouting. Then a horn sounded as Christopher dropped his shovel and ran out of sight.

"Christopher?" Charlotte hobbled to the back door as fast as she could.

Chapter
Twelve

B ill!" Charlotte looked around the corner of Eulalia Barry's little back porch to see her elder son sitting in his silver Toyota, mired up to its hubcaps, wheels spinning and mud flinging in all directions. He'd obviously tried to follow a tractor in but had slipped off the gravel drive.

Bill threw up a hand in disgust as he gunned the motor, but that didn't help free him.

Pete sloshed up to the car and waved his hands, signaling for Bill to stop spinning his wheels and making such a mess. Bill didn't normally or willingly take instructions from his younger brother, so he gunned the motor even more. This of course sprayed mud and water in a shower over Pete's head.

Unperturbed, Pete turned away and held tightly to the hood of his rain slicker for as long as his brother spun his wheels. As the sandbaggers watched, Bill finally gave up and slammed his hands on his steering wheel. Bill could certainly make a scene when he wanted to.

"You done?" Pete drawled, a grin slipping across his face. By this time their father had arrived to see what all the commotion was about.

"Pete," said Bob, stepping into the clear from behind a tractor. "What's going on here?"

There was no need to explain; Pete simply waved at his brother's mud-encrusted car as several sandbaggers gathered around to watch the show.

The driver's-side power window edged down a few inches, and Bill's red face peered out at them. "I had a heck of a time finding you guys," he told them.

"No kidding?" answered Pete.

"That's right. Nobody was home when I went to check. So then I'm driving by, out there on the road, and I see all these tractors."

"Well then, you found us all right." Pete wiped the mud from his cheek with the back of his hand. "So what were you doing out this way in the first place?"

"Had to check with emergency services in Bedford. We share resources between towns."

"Looks like you coulda shared some resources out our way, huh?"

"Look, Pete, this isn't the only place that's in trouble."

No one said anything else; perhaps the sight of the bogged-down Toyota was enough entertainment to go around.

"So how about pulling me out of this mess?" Bill asked.

By that time Dave Meyers had pulled up behind the Toyota with his backhoe, just inches away from taking off Bill's bumper. Dave hopped out of his rig to see who had blocked the driveway.

"No time to be messing around with fools and tourists," yelled Dave, making no attempt at diplomacy. He adjusted the visor of his muddy John Deere cap and leaned in for a better look.

"Oh, it's you, huh, Bill?" A tiny smile crossed his face as he shook his head. "Haven't seen you out this way for a while. And then on a day like today? Good timing."

"Yeah, well . . ." Bill still hadn't dared open his door, perhaps because of the rain, perhaps because the locals hadn't offered a warm welcome. "My mistake. Mom, are you all right?"

Charlotte waved her thanks at him.

"We're perfectly fine, Bill. I'm just worried about you now. You just get out of here before your car's swallowed up."

Actually, she wasn't exaggerating. The rising waters had crept around the sandbag perimeter to lap at their feet while runoff from up the hill washed down the gullies Bill's car wheels had created. He probably could not have chosen a worse place or a worse time to get stuck if he'd tried.

"Actually," he answered, "I do need to get back. My fire chief back in River Bend is going to be looking for me."

"All right then." Now Bob took charge, and Pete uncoiled a length of chain from a toolbox bolted to the back of their older tractor. "Appreciate your coming out, Bill."

Without a word, Pete dove into the mud behind his big brother's car with the end of the chain in hand. Meanwhile Bob maneuvered their tractor around, ready to pull the little vehicle clear, backside first.

A minute later, Pete emerged from beneath the car and nodded at his father, who slowly eased out the tractor's clutch and took up the slack. "Don't want to see that chain snap in our faces," he said.

"Don't gun it!" yelled Bob, but even so, Bill spun his wheels a bit too desperately and sprayed the onlookers with a little more mud.

Meanwhile the deep ruts did not seem to want to give up their captive; the mud made giant and considerable sucking noises as it seemed to pull the little car back. Bob revved up his tractor in response, straining the chain for a long, uncertain moment before the Toyota finally popped out of its hole and rolled free. Dave thumped on the car's hood while Pete disconnected the chain.

"Now get out of here while you can," Dave told Bill, who nodded gravely.

"I'll take the back road," he said. "Dad, tell Mom we'll be back to help with your open house."

"I heard that, Bill." Charlotte leaned over the porch railing. "You just drive carefully and don't worry about me. We'll call you later."

She winced as the pain shot through her lower back once more, but did her best not to react. She waved at her son as he plowed through a muddy wash on his way back up the hill. He would turn right, away from Bedford, and take the longer way back home to River Bend.

Praying he would make it without further drama or mishap, she leaned against the house for support as she tried to relax her back. Down in the mud, the men had gathered everyone around their three remaining tractors and one backhoe.

"Let's see what we can do about giving the Barrys a

hand," said Bob, sounding a bit like a coach talking to his team at halftime. He turned to look up at Charlotte on the porch with a quizzical look.

"You really okay there?" he asked.

She forced a smile and nodded before looking back at Mrs. Barry, who was rearranging her curtains once again.

"I'll be fine," she told him, raising her voice against the wind. Bob hurried toward her as she lowered herself to the steps, gripping the railing tightly. She slipped and might have fallen if Bob hadn't caught her by the elbow.

"I don't think you're okay." He didn't loosen his grip. "I shouldn't have let you come here."

"Nonsense," she countered. "Who would have helped Hannah . . . or Mrs. Barry? I told you, I'm—"

"That's enough, Char." He cut her off and steered her to the tractor.

"Don't tell me that's enough," she answered him impatiently. "You asked, and I'm telling you. I'm fine now, and I can decide if I'm not."

Bob continued with her toward the tractor as he called to the others standing nearby. "We're going for more sand," he told them. "Emily, how about you come along with your grandma? She could probably use some help back at the house."

Emily didn't argue, just grimly wiped the mud from her cheek and nodded as she joined them. Pete stepped over to help them up into the utility trailer while Charlotte did all she could not to wince in pain as she stepped aboard.

"Dad, you want to hurry back," Pete said as he pulled his

father aside. "We still have four more farms along this stretch of river, and not much time."

No one needed the reminder, but Bob nodded as he started up the tractor once more. He checked the box of generator parts he had borrowed from Frank before they left the Carters' place.

"Back before you know it," he replied as Charlotte and Emily each found a place to sit near the front of the trailer. "Just gotta get that generator fired up back home, and we'll be good to go."

Charlotte decided being stubborn was probably not going to help her this time. Instead she sat in the trailer and braced herself for the inevitable bone-jarring bumps.

"Keep an eye on those boys," she told Pete, who waved and nodded.

"Don't worry about us," he told her with a jaunty salute. "You just take care of yourself."

Take care of herself? It seemed so much more natural to be taking care of others. Taking care of herself seemed so . . . well, so selfish.

As they headed back through the flood in the direction of home she felt a lump growing in her throat. She gripped the trailer sides with white knuckles to keep from being jostled about. She was thankful Bob's tractor could pull them safely through floodwaters that would have swallowed most cars. Even as the rising water gurgled just beneath them and lapped at the sides of the trailer, she knew her husband would get them home safely. And up on the rise, far enough away from the raging creek, her home would surely be fine. At least she hoped it was.

When she stopped to think about it, however, she couldn't bear the thought of Hannah and Frank losing their lovely home next to the creek. And now she'd left poor Mrs. Barry, bustling about in her little house, frightened and confused, with floodwaters rising all around and the terrified cat trapped in its box above the refrigerator. Had they done the right thing, leaving those poor people behind?

"Bob!" she shouted. It took two or three yells to get his attention. "We should have brought the Barrys with us, don't you think? Bob? We need to turn around."

But Bob shook his head and kept their tractor headed up the gravel drive. Rivulets washed between their wheels, slowing their progress.

"Dick's not going to leave his place," Bob called back over his shoulder.

"You asked him?"

"Didn't need to."

Charlotte sighed and bit her tongue before she said something she might later regret. But . . . Bob could be so stubborn too! Maybe she could have convinced Mrs. Barry to come with them, at least.

"If it gets worse," he went on, "you know we'll go back in and get them."

Though she would never admit it at this point, perhaps Bob was right. They could go back later. She relaxed just a bit, but when the trailer hit a bump she automatically winced. Emily leaned a little closer and held on to her arm.

"They're going to be okay, Grandma," Emily told her. The reassurance sounded just a bit odd, coming from her granddaughter. She did, however, sound a lot like her Uncle Pete.

A COUPLE OF HOURS LATER Charlotte had to admit she felt better in her own home wearing a clean set of dry clothes, sitting in her rocking chair with Toby at her feet.

But when Emily came down the stairs to check on her, she frowned. "You don't look so good, Grandma."

Certainly Charlotte hadn't looked completely well during the ride home, but did she look worse now?

"My back is acting up."

"No wonder, lifting all those sandbags."

By this time their generator was humming out back, providing their well and pump with its much-needed pressure. With the right part in hand, Bob must have made quick work of the repair. In any case, the electric light in the kitchen now cast a cheery glow that made Charlotte want to curl up with a book and a cup of hot coffee, despite everything going on around them. Better to start coffee for Bob and Pete; they'd be chilled to the bone when they finally made it home—by dinnertime, she hoped, the way Bob had promised before he headed back to the sandbagging rescues.

But apparently Emily had other ideas, and she grabbed a slicker from the coat tree by the back door.

"You're not going out there again," said Charlotte.

Emily didn't hesitate. "We need to check the barn," she answered. "The horses. Just to be sure they're okay."

Charlotte studied the concern in her granddaughter's expression, the pleading in her face, and she sighed.

"All right, then. I'll go with you."

A few minutes later Charlotte had no idea how the heavens had not been wrung dry. All she knew was that despite their raingear, both of them had been thoroughly soaked by wind-driven rain before they'd even made it across the gravel courtyard between house and barn.

The good news was that the barn had not been blown down. The worst damage was that several boards had come loose, allowing some hay to get wet and creating a little bit of a muddy mess along a couple of outside walls.

Without too much trouble Charlotte and Emily were able to move Stormy, Shania, Princess, Tom, and Ben to drier stalls away from the damaged wall, where a steady dripping made things soggy but not unbearable. Emily cooed a soft assurance to the old mare, Britney, as a couple more loose boards slammed in the wind and the relentless rain sounded on the overhead metal roof like a snare drum.

"You're just like your mother with that horse."

Charlotte startled herself with the words and the unbidden memory of her daughter's horse, but the resemblance couldn't be avoided.

Emily looked up from stroking Britney's mane. "Why don't you ever tell me more stories about Mom? I want to hear them, you know. I mean, even if they . . ."

Even if they hurt. Emily's voice caught for a moment, and Charlotte wasn't quite sure how to answer. Could Emily really understand the pain of losing a daughter? Perhaps she could. . . .

"Well, Emily, you know she spent an awful lot of time out here. Grooming that horse, cleaning up. I would come out to check on her at night, and she would still be here, sometimes reading the horse her diary like it was her best friend."

"*Hmm.*" Emily smiled weakly as she ran her finger across the worn, cracked leather of an old bridle hanging on the barn wall. She guessed her mother had once used it.

"In fact," Charlotte went on, "I remember her fifteenth birthday, I think it was, when her friends had to go out and find her. Of course your mom was out here, brushing that horse."

"On her birthday?"

Charlotte nodded, the memory bringing her back to the present. "Speaking of which, you know your grandfather and I wanted to do something special for you this weekend, but with all this flooding . . ."

"It doesn't matter." Emily was a little too quick to answer.

"Yes, it does. And I hope you're not disappointed. I was thinking perhaps you'd like to invite a friend or two over for dinner, and, you know, I was planning to bake a cake. They'd be welcome to sleep over, if you like."

Emily sighed and nodded as she turned away, back toward the door. "Sure, Grandma. That's fine."

Charlotte followed, feeling a bit of an ache in her heart at the disappointment in Emily's voice. But whether the girl's feelings were dampened by the memory of her mother or by the thoughts of the scaled-down birthday party, Charlotte couldn't be sure. In any case, she knew she would need to get back to the kitchen soon. When the men came home, they were certainly going to be hungry.

Chapter
Thirteen

Back inside the house, Charlotte pushed aside a small mound of Farm Family of the Year paperwork, along with a list she had started of things she needed to do and buy before the big day—which she hadn't actually thought about during the past twenty-four hours. Goodness, preparing for the Farm Family open house was the very last thing she wanted to worry about right now. Her back was feeling better, but it was far from healed and she had to be careful how she moved.

She thought of tossing the paperwork in the trash can under the sink, and wouldn't that make Bob happy, to just forget the whole thing? Instead she stacked it high on the top shelf of her pantry, out of the way and out of sight. For now. She would face that decision later.

"Emily!" she called, turning back to the present. "I need some help in here. We're going to make spaghetti."

Emily turned from the living room window, where she had been watching the rain. Strange. Charlotte had seen quite enough of the cloudburst that seemed so endlessly fascinating to her granddaughter.

"I can't believe it just keeps coming down," Emily told her, "like some kind of monsoon."

Monsoon was a good word for it, as the heavy rains had not abated now for . . . how long? Somewhere behind all the inky clouds, the sun had probably set. Charlotte squinted at the wall clock just to be sure though. "That's not right," she said, puzzled.

"Grandma." Consulting her wristwatch, Emily stepped over to the plug-in clock and twisted the stem on the side of its face. "It's been out for sixteen hours, you know."

"Oh. Yes, of course."

Bob's generator supplied enough power to the kitchen for Charlotte to cook with, and the large gas tank Bob had fitted to the machine meant they didn't even have to worry about refueling it for several hours. Now, in the kitchen, Emily turned to face her with her hands on her hips. "What do you want me to do?" she asked.

Charlotte dug out one of her large aluminum kettles from a lower cabinet and handed it to her.

"Let's fill this with water and start it to boiling. I'll have you take care of the pasta while I cook the hamburger. And whoever finishes first can make the sauce."

"Okay, Grandma." The two worked in unison, and they didn't have to wait long for the hungry workers to arrive. As Charlotte set six places at the table, she thought she heard the distant chugging of a tractor, or perhaps two. Emily dropped her spoon directly on the stove, ignoring the ceramic cow-shaped spoon rest, and hurried to the living room window to check as Toby barked from the porch.

"It's them!" she said. Charlotte joined her to see a single set of headlights coming through the soggy twilight. Another set followed the first, bouncing in the darkness.

"Well." Charlotte straightened up, looking from the steamy kitchen and back to the two oncoming tractors. "Here come the troops."

Emily smiled as they returned to the kitchen to set out more plates, napkins, and silverware. Presently the sound of tractor engines sputtered to a stop just outside the back door, replaced by loud voices as the army burst through the back door.

"Boots off!" Charlotte ordered before Pete had a chance to track mud into the house. He should know better. The driving rain followed him inside, and so did Bob, Sam, and Christopher, all looking half-drowned and worse for wear.

"Let's get them some towels!" Charlotte said as she helped Bob remove his rain slicker. A moment later her granddaughter returned with an armload. They unrolled a couple by the door where the boys could pile their wet gear, used a couple more as mops on the linoleum, and handed out the rest to the boys for drying off.

"I'm glad you made it home," Charlotte told them.

"Just a quick break," said Bob, checking out the window, "and then we've got to get right back. Nobody else has power either."

"I'm going back too," said Christopher, rainwater dripping off his nose. Charlotte and Bob shook their heads in concert.

"You've already been a big help," Bob told him. "But your grandma needs you here now."

"No, she doesn't. What am I supposed to do here? Our house isn't going to flood like the Carter place."

Charlotte gave her husband a quick look to be sure, but Bob's frown told her Christopher might not be too far off target. The Carter place had to be in serious danger.

"Like I said, you're staying here, and we're going back. That's all there is to it."

"That's not fair!"

When Christopher's eyes blazed Charlotte couldn't help seeing Denise as a teenager, using the same line on them when something didn't go her way. (Which, as it turned out, was nearly every day.) Back then, Denise could draw her father into a heated exchange just about anytime she cared to. For a moment Charlotte thought she would see a replay, here and now. Instead, the anger in Bob's eyes flared briefly, and then flickered out.

"I'm not going to discuss this with you, Christopher." Bob's voice steadied. "So you can either think about it up in your room, or you can settle down and have dinner with us. What'll it be?"

This time there was no way to argue, so Christopher just crossed his arms and pouted quietly in his chair while Pete leaned over the stove to poke a finger in the sauce for a sample.

Any other time Charlotte would have swatted him. But she held back when she saw the grim look of exhaustion on her husband's face. Bob's eyelids drooped as if he wanted nothing more than to collapse into bed. He looked up with a tired expression as he fell into a chair at the dinner table.

"Perhaps you could take some supper back for the others." Charlotte said. "We've made plenty."

"Yeah," agreed Pete. "You must have thought we were going to be pretty darn hungry or something."

"Emily and I just wanted to be prepared. We'll put it in some plastic containers for you."

Bob simply nodded his thanks, but his eyelids drooped even more as he glanced back at Charlotte. "That's fine. Would you say grace for us tonight?" he said.

Actually, she had never stopped praying ever since all this began. But tonight she didn't mind specifically thanking God, first for the meal, and also "for the neighbors, Lord, who have worked so hard to keep others safe."

When Charlotte squeezed her eyes shut she could see the good, honest faces of the farm families she knew and loved. Only now, their expressions were etched with the pain and mud of these past difficult days. She paused before continuing. "And we lift up Hannah and Frank, Lord, and their family. Please give them the strength they need. And the Barrys, especially poor Mrs. Barry. Father, please comfort her. And all those whose farms are threatened, whose homes are too close to the flooding. Please protect them."

Heaven only knew those families could use more help than Charlotte and her family could offer. When she'd finished praying, Bob's head nodded before he rubbed his eyes and picked up a fork.

"Amen." His voice sounded hoarse and far away. Was he really as exhausted as he looked?

"Bob," she told him, ladling up a generous portion of pasta, "maybe you'd better rest here for a few minutes after dinner. After all—"

"No." He wolfed down another bite, speaking with his

mouth full. "I told them we'd be right back with more sand. The Carters are in trouble if the water keeps coming up. We've got to put another row of bags on their wall."

So Christopher was right. They ate in silence for a minute while Bob and Pete stuffed buttered French bread in their mouths and chugged down a couple of glasses of milk apiece. Sam followed their lead. Then, before long, Bob pushed back his chair.

"You haven't been here five minutes!" Charlotte knew that even if she objected, it wouldn't change a thing. "At least have some dessert."

"No time, but thanks." Bob grabbed another piece of unbuttered bread and stuffed it into the pocket of his rain slicker, where it would surely turn to mush the moment he went outside. He turned to Pete to discuss how much sand they could load, where they could get more bags, and which farm needed the most help and soonest. Charlotte couldn't remember a time when Bob had left the dinner table without having first read from the Scriptures or at least a story Bible.

"I'll drive one of the tractors back, Grandpa," Sam volunteered as they pulled their still-dripping raincoats back on and stepped into their muddy boots at the back door.

Bob hesitated and looked toward the shelf where they kept the Bible, but he didn't say no right away. Meanwhile Pete grabbed an armload of the plastic containers Charlotte had filled with dinner servings and stuffed them into plastic shopping bags. Charlotte added a handful of plastic forks and knives, and wondered if she should go back with them as well.

"Thanks, Mom." Pete squeezed his mother's shoulder. "We needed that. How's your back, by the way?"

Charlotte wasn't in the mood to go into details, and she wasn't going to tell him how much it still hurt. "Never mind me. Your father . . ." She lowered her voice and pulled Pete aside as Bob headed out the door first. "I'm concerned about him. Is he doing okay? He looks so exhausted."

"No more'n the rest of us, Mom. There's people out there who have been working on the sandbagging lines since late last night."

They all had to be at least as wet and miserable as Bob, Pete, and Sam were. Those poor men, Charlotte thought. It really didn't seem to matter how much raingear they wore; they would be wet and muddy no matter what.

"You just take care of your father and Sam," she said.

"I think you told me that before." Pete smiled at her. "But I will, and you still need to take care of yourself. Don't worry. Everything's under control."

She was about to say that everything most certainly *was not* under control, but decided against it. He kissed her cheek, leaving a smudge of mud on her face. She gently rubbed it away as her men left once more. Then she glanced back at the table, where her littlest man sat scowling, his elbows parked next to his half-finished plate of spaghetti—normally one of his favorites—and gazed through the storm to a place far away.

"I'm proud of you," she told him. "You were really helping the men down there at the neighbors' farms."

Tears welled up in Christopher's eyes, and his lip quivered as he turned away. "Then why won't they let me help now?"

His chair toppled to the floor as he bolted out of the kitchen, but she didn't call after him and didn't try to stop him. Not this time. Her back would probably have gone out again if she'd tried to bend over anyway. So she just stood there as he stormed up the stairs.

Actually, she could have bawled herself.

Chapter
Fourteen

Charlotte looked up from one of her favorite books of Robert Frost poetry, which she'd been trying to read by candlelight, and realized she'd been scanning the same poem for several minutes, reading and re-reading lines about springtime that she could not seem to wrap her mind around.

Not that Frost's lovely verses were beyond her, not usually. She gave it another try.

"Oh, give us pleasure in the flowers today," she read out loud, but all she could think of were the flowers in her yard that had been drowned and destroyed by this flood—even the plants she and Emily had brought from the nursery in Harding. Perhaps she wasn't in the mood for poetry after all.

She glanced down at the rug, where Toby was dreaming a dog-dream, quivering and shaking her paws. The dog sighed and let out a muffled woof.

"Chasing a bird, girl?"

Who could say? The old grandfather clock kept on ticking, but all Charlotte could feel was guilt for not doing anything useful. At least the old heirloom hadn't been stopped by the power outage.

Eight-fifteen, and they still aren't home.

By nine Charlotte had worn a track in the carpet beneath the living room window. She was stiff-legged because of her aching back but determined to see when the men were returning. She leaned against the window frame, avoiding the flickering candle flame, and wondered what the two kids were doing up in their rooms. In the dark, no less.

"Emily?" She finally called up the stairs. "Christopher? Can either of you see anything from your windows?"

No one answered, so she tried again a little louder. A gust of wind rattled the windows in reply.

A moment later the dim beam of a flashlight shone down the stairwell at her, making her jump.

"You can come up here to my room, Grandma," Christopher called down.

"Can you see?"

"It's dark, but I think I can see when they come back."

Charlotte considered what it would take for her to climb the stairs right now. She reached around to feel her back, and decided against it. Good thing her bedroom was on the main floor.

"Tell you what," she said. "You come down here, and we'll watch through the living room window. Maybe we can pop some popcorn while we wait."

That brought him down. A few minutes later the smell of freshly popped corn lured Emily down for a peek, as well.

"Want some?" Christopher stuffed another handful in his mouth as he pointed his flashlight at the yard beyond the window. "Grandma put extra melted butter on it."

"Maybe just a little." Emily scooped up a few kernels and

stood with them by the window, shifting uncertainly. No one said anything but Charlotte could almost feel the cloud of worry hanging over their heads.

"I know." Christopher finally spoke up as if he had a grand idea, and he held up his finger. "We could call Sam's cell phone. He might answer."

"I thought of that," replied Emily, frowning. She set the mostly empty popcorn bowl on the nearby coffee table, out of the way. "I saw it up on his dresser."

"Oh. That means he can't answer, I guess."

"You're a genius."

Christopher ignored the jab and returned to pressing his nose against the window, adding little round grease smudges that would need to be cleaned off later, but not now. Again no one said anything for several minutes as they stared into the rainy darkness, illuminated only by the weak yellow pool of light from their window.

Behind them, the old grandfather clock kept time in the shadows, chiming ten times over the sound of the wind. Still no one said anything about going to bed, and Charlotte wasn't going to be the first to mention it.

"What if they fell into the creek?" Christopher finally asked, working his way to the bottom of the bowl.

Charlotte shivered at the thought.

"Of course they haven't fallen into the creek." She hoped saying the words out loud might help her to stop worrying about the very same thing. "They'll be home any minute; you wait and see."

"Is that them?" Emily interrupted. At first Charlotte wasn't sure, but when she squinted she could make out the bouncing headlights once more, and she breathed a silent prayer of thanks.

"What did I tell you?" She couldn't help clapping her hands as they watched the lights approach. "Everyone's coming home. Everyone's fine."

As they were to find out, however, everyone was not fine. Bob's dark expression as he pushed in through the back door told her as much.

"Bob?" she asked, helping him shrug off his raingear. "What happened to you?"

One of the sleeves had been shredded, but his wet, muddy plaid shirt underneath looked okay.

"I thought we were going to be able to hold it back," he mumbled, kicking his boots to the corner and heading for the pot of coffee Charlotte had left simmering.

That was it? Obviously he wasn't answering any more questions at this point, but Charlotte had a sinking feeling she knew exactly what he was talking about—especially when she recognized another voice coming in out of the rain with Pete.

"Hannah?"

Charlotte's best friend stood framed in the doorway for a moment, dripping and hesitating as she pushed back the hood of her poncho. Like the men, she looked beaten, bruised, and muddy. She burst into tears the moment she saw Charlotte.

"Oh, honey." Charlotte limped over to give her a hug, poncho and all. Hannah buried her sobs in Charlotte's soft shoulder. "Come on in; let's dry you off. Whatever happened, everything's going to be all right."

Charlotte wished she believed her own words as Pete filed in right behind Hannah, wearing the same defeated expression as his father and carrying a pair of wet black suitcases. A grim-faced Frank came next while Sam brought up the rear and closed the door behind him. Hannah couldn't seem to stop sobbing; Frank quietly accepted a steaming cup of coffee from Bob.

"I'm sorry." Hannah finally backed away and wiped her tears with the back of her hand. All Charlotte could find to offer her was a napkin from the little holder on the table.

"Please, Hannah. No need to apologize." Charlotte looked to Bob for the official explanation, and he sighed as he gripped his coffee mug between two hands.

"It was holding for a while," he finally told her, his voice so low and quiet she had to strain to hear him. "But then it started rising so fast, nobody could do anything. I think maybe a snag downstream somewhere had backed it up."

It. The creek.

"Like, over the top." With his hands Pete pantomimed the flood of water cascading over the top of the sandbags like one of Sam's California waves. "There was nothing we could do about it. After all that work."

Pete looked to be almost in tears himself as he continued the story.

"The whole lower level of the house, just like that." He snapped his fingers. "Dry one minute, knee-deep the next. Never seen anything like it. I just hope it doesn't get much higher."

"Was it still rising?" Charlotte said, hating to ask the question. Pete shrugged his shoulders.

"We couldn't stick around to find out. If we had, maybe even the tractors wouldn't have gotten us out of there."

"Oh, no." Charlotte winced, even though she had expected the news. Hannah's tears brought more tears of her own. The two women clung to each other as Bob added his perspective.

"Good news is we got most of the furniture up the stairs to the second floor already. Pretty much cleared out everything 'cept the carpets and the heavier stuff. Even so . . . it's a mess, with water getting into the walls. I told them they needed to stay with us for a while. Their place wouldn't be safe for anybody, at least until the water drops back down."

"Of course." Charlotte nodded. "We have plenty of room. But Hannah, I'm so sorry. This is—"

"We're okay." Frank interrupted her, but gently. "The main thing is nobody's hurt, and . . . and you guys worked so hard to set up those sandbags. I'll never forget what you did."

"Maybe so, Frank." Bob took another sip of hot coffee. "But it turned out to be a waste. We couldn't stop the water."

"What are you, Superman? Wasn't no waste, and it's not like it's your fault."

"If we'd been there a little earlier . . ."

"Would you stop blaming yourself for something you can't help?" Frank raised his voice for emphasis. "And listen, we'll only be here a couple of days. We don't want to put you out."

"Nonsense." Charlotte kept an arm around Hannah as she led her in the direction of the stairs. "You can stay here just as long as you need to. Nobody's going to worry about that. Now let's get you cleaned up and dried out. You know where the bathroom is upstairs, and we'll put out some clean towels for you. We still only have power here in the kitchen and then out on some of the equipment, but there are plenty of candles to go around."

"Shoulda wired that differently," said Bob, shaking his head. "But I'm not sure the generator could handle more."

"It's fine." Charlotte wished she could reassure him more. "Emily, would you please show Hannah upstairs? She and Frank can stay in the spare bedroom. Sam and Christopher, why don't you help them with their things?"

"We didn't have much time to pack," Hannah admitted, referring to the small suitcases the boys now carried. "Just what we could grab. Everything happened so fast."

"I know." Charlotte nodded her understanding and switched on a flashlight for them. "I'm just sorry I wasn't there to help."

"You really couldn't have done anything, Charlotte." Hannah shook her head. "Just like they couldn't do anything to hold back Heather Creek."

Charlotte looked over at Bob.

"You think there are others?" she asked. "What about the Barrys? What about downstream?"

"Mr. Barry's nephew from Harding came and fetched 'em . . . and the cat. But downstream?" He looked as if he could barely hold his eyes open. "Hard to know. Plenty of fields are flooded, that's for sure. We'll know more by daylight."

"Well, nobody's hurt," added Hannah, "And we're together. That's the important . . ." Her voice choked and she couldn't finish her sentence, so Frank added his thanks and said something about getting cleaned up. Before they reached the foot of the stairs, though, Hannah stopped short.

"Wait just a minute, Sam," she said. "I need to get something out of my suitcase, if you don't mind."

When Sam dutifully returned with her small suitcase she unzipped a bulging outer pocket, pulled out a quart-sized plastic bag, and came back to the kitchen with it.

"I baked these the other day," she told them, looking a little sheepish, "before the power went out. I'm just sorry they got a little squished."

"Oh, that doesn't matter a bit," Charlotte answered as quickly as she could. "Anything you bake always tastes wonderful."

Charlotte accepted the gift, though what had apparently been a dozen muffins now more closely resembled a large smashed pancake. For now she didn't want to attempt extricating this crumbly mess out of the bag, at least not in front of Hannah. So she smiled and placed it on the table for later.

Meanwhile, the Carters turned to follow Sam once again, leaving Bob, Charlotte, and Pete to stand awkwardly in the kitchen.

"Well," said Bob, "guess this means your open house isn't going to happen."

Charlotte avoided her husband's look as she poured another cup of coffee and handed it to Pete.

"Decaf." Charlotte couldn't think of anything else to say, so she repeated a trite-sounding chestnut about how everything would turn out fine, and how they did what they could.

Pete stared at the cup, swirled it around before taking a sip, and then set it back down on the table.

"Wasn't enough," he told them, heading for the door once again. The drawn look on his face told them more than Charlotte wanted to know. "I'll be in my apartment."

⌣ Chapter
Fifteen

S am thought he was dreaming as he swatted at the insect that had grabbed him by the shoulders.

"Get away from me!" he mumbled, pulling himself free.

But the insect wouldn't give up. It even laid a hand on Sam's mouth as his head cleared.

"Shh!" said the insect, which had somehow turned into Uncle Pete crouching by Sam's bed—though it was still pretty dark to see exactly who it was.

If it was the next day, thought Sam, it should have been light. And if it wasn't light, he wasn't ready to get up. How long past midnight had it been when they finally made it to bed? And now this? He tried to roll over, but Uncle Pete wouldn't let him.

"Need some help, dude." Uncle Pete shook his shoulder until Sam had to face him with a groan.

"What time is it?"

"Doesn't matter. I've been listening to my scanner, and we need to go help."

"What about Grandpa?" Sam squinted in the direction of his alarm clock but saw nothing except shadows. That could only mean the power was still out. *Great.*

"He's still in bed. You saw him last night, didn't you? He's spent, and I don't want him getting a heart attack. Besides, there's not enough room in the boat."

Sam sat straight up at that.

"The boat? What are you talking about?"

"Get your pants on, and let's go."

Sam did as he was told, fumbling around in the half-light for a dry pair of socks. He followed Pete out of his room and slipped down the stairs after his uncle.

"Are you going to—" He corrected his voice down to a whisper when Uncle Pete signaled with a finger to his lips. "I mean, are you going to tell me what we're doing?"

But Uncle Pete was already pulling on his raingear and heading out the back door. He stopped for a moment to adjust a portable radio clipped to his belt, a police-type scanner that squawked with an occasional harsh voice that Sam couldn't understand.

A hastily scrawled note on the kitchen table said, "Pete and Sam went out to pull some animals out of the water. Back by lunch." Sam guessed he would find out what they were really doing soon enough.

If he could catch up, that is. He trotted through the dark drizzle, wondering how he had been talked into crawling out of his warm bed this early. Out in a corner of the machine shed, Uncle Pete yanked off a dusty tarp and pulled a dented old aluminum skiff out of the shadows. Sam caught a corner. They dragged it out into the rain, then onto the trailer they'd been pulling behind one of the tractors.

"We going fishing?" Sam tried to stay light, but already Uncle Pete had turned back to the shed.

"You could say that."

Next stop was a far corner behind a long workbench, where Grandpa stashed old tools and machine parts, stuff he didn't know what to do with but couldn't throw away. With the help of a flashlight, Uncle Pete dug around in a pile of engine stuff until he locked on to something and pulled.

"Don't just stand there looking," he grunted at Sam. "Pull on that handle."

As it turned out, "that handle" was connected to a greasy old aluminum machine of some sort, which they yanked on until they got it free of all the other junk. A propeller on the end of a shaft told Sam it had to be an outboard motor—though he had never seen anything so old. Along with a couple of old oars, they brought it out to the the main doorway, where Uncle Pete could get a closer look with a flashlight. Sam thought it said "Evinrude" under a thick layer of dust and grease, but this thing should have been in a museum.

"Used to run like a champ," said Uncle Pete, poking at the wires and unscrewing the cap to its built-in gas tank.

"When was that?"

"Uh, let me think . . ." Uncle Pete scratched his chin. "Guess I was still in high school last time Dad took me out fishing on Crystal Lake. Maybe that was a few years ago."

"A few years ago?" Sam couldn't believe it. "And you think it's still going to work?"

"Sure it is. These things are bulletproof. Throw it in the trailer with those oars while I find some gas."

Now Sam really had his doubts. But since Uncle Pete sounded so sure of himself, well . . . A couple of minutes later they both clambered up on the tractor, and Sam held on as they rumbled down the soggy driveway.

"So here's the thing." Uncle Pete shouted above the roar of the tractor's engine. "Radio said there are reports of some livestock stranded in a field just south of here. We're going to go check it out, see if we can help."

"Right." Sam was starting to feel a little bit like a Coast Guard rescue pilot, complete with scanner radio, hovering over the devastation of a flooded city—the way he'd seen on the news. A glitter of standing water in many of the fields on either side of the road added to the feeling. Only this was no city, and their tractor was no Coast Guard chopper.

Once they'd pulled out of their driveway and onto Heather Creek Road they would have no traffic to worry about as they headed south toward the Carter place and the worst of the flooding.

"Over there!" After several minutes, Sam pointed to a flooded field on the Heather Creek side of the road, a downslope with a rise in the middle that formed a small island. Its sole occupant: an obviously distressed sheep.

"Tell me how it got itself stuck out there, huh?" Sam hopped off to prepare their rescue boat.

"Are we actually going to put that in the boat?" Sam had seen sheep turned loose in a barnyard before. Uncle Pete grinned and held up a short length of rope he'd stashed in the trailer.

"You're looking at the eighth grade sheep-wrangling champion of Adams County. Come on. Let's get this boat in the water."

Sam helped his uncle wrangle the blunt-nosed aluminum skiff off the trailer, and together they shoved it over the muddy grass and into the cold, knee-deep water. From there they mounted the old outboard, Uncle Pete gassed it up, and after some fiddling he yanked on the cord.

Nothing.

"*Hmm.*" He fiddled some more. "No reason it shouldn't fire right up."

After several more tries, though, the best he could manage was a halfhearted wheeze and a couple of coughs. Sam thought maybe he could get a better angle at it if he climbed into the boat.

"Let me try," he said. And though he'd never actually started a motor like this by himself, he copied what he'd seen Uncle Pete do, and gave it a mighty tug.

No one had warned him what would happen if it actually did start, however. He was nearly launched over the back end of the boat as the little outboard roared to life and the skiff lurched forward, out into deeper water. Sam hugged the outboard and tried to steer.

"What do I do?" he hollered back at Uncle Pete, who had been left at the water's edge. Uncle Pete made a big sweeping motion and yelled something back. After a little trial and error, Sam managed to throttle down and circle back to where his uncle waited.

"Stop the engine!" yelled Uncle Pete, but Sam still wasn't quite sure of the controls. Instead he managed to beach his aluminum whale with the engine still running. Good enough. Uncle Pete hopped aboard, took over the controls, and soon the rescue mission was back on.

"All right," said Uncle Pete. "Now when we get to that little rise, that island, I want you to jump out and tackle the sheep. You hold him, and I'll tie up his legs, and we'll bring him back aboard the boat. He'll drown if he stays out there."

Or starve, maybe. Sam had heard how notoriously helpless a sheep could be. Still, once they'd landed and he'd carried out his assignment, he wasn't quite prepared for its kick when he launched into the flying tackle.

"Hold on!" yelled Uncle Pete.

Easy for him to say. Sam felt himself being dragged around the little island, hardly more than ten or fifteen feet across. But he didn't let go of the sheep's leg as it grunted and brayed and made all its other terrified-sheep sounds. He didn't blame the poor thing. He just wished they'd had a better plan.

Fortunately, Pete was as good with his piece of rope as his boast, and he quickly had all four legs hogtied before Sam could get up out of the mud.

"There," he said. "That wasn't so hard, was it?"

The sheep settled down as they dragged the soaking bundle of wool over to the boat. Then they were off again, a bit lower in the water but headed for the nearest barn, where Sam could make out a few people in the distance. He grinned back at his uncle from his perch in the bow.

"So where's our next rescue?"

They didn't have to go far as they crisscrossed fields adjacent to the creek, looking for stranded livestock. During the next several hours they pulled seven more sheep to safety— all of them clueless, unaware of the danger they were in. The rescuers also managed to snag two young calves that were desperate to get back to their mothers, and they cautiously approached a goat tangled in a half-submerged barbed-wired fence. This would prove their toughest rescue yet.

"Dude!" Sam leaned over the bow for a better look. "How did he get himself into that mess?"

Uncle Pete slowed the motor. In the past hour or so the steady rain had turned nasty once more, unleashing another downpour that seemed to instantly swell the flood. Where the waters had once reached halfway up a line of fenceposts, now the waves lapped to within inches of the top.

The large black-and-white goat thrashed and cried out as they closed the gap, sometimes disappearing completely beneath the surface while it kicked up a frothy foam in the coffee-colored water—sort of like a latte from an espresso machine.

But there was no time for thinking of coffee. With the water rising again—and quickly—they might have only one chance. Sam looked back at his uncle, who nodded at him.

"Careful, Sam. I don't want to have to come in after you."

Well, Sam didn't want that either. But as the boat edged up to the fence line he slipped over the side, gasping momentarily at the numbing cold of the water that instantly filled his boots and reached up to his chest.

"It's deeper, here!" He called back as he reached out to free the panicked animal. Standing in the churning water, he couldn't help thinking of how he had fished that little girl, Daisy, out of the creek just the month before.

And though this wasn't a little girl, now he had a new challenge. In a moment he could see the problem all too clearly: A broken strand of wire had wrapped around the goat's front leg, the barbs digging deeper, like a fish hook, with each movement. Uncle Pete reached over and held Sam's shoulders as Sam tried to untangle the thrashing mess. The goat looked straight up at Sam with its odd, sideways pupils, braying and kicking with all its might.

"Don't let him kick you!" Uncle Pete didn't need to warn him. Sam had the end of the wire in his hand, and he unwound and untwisted it as best he could. One more turn, and . . .

For one terrifying moment Sam felt his footing slip from underneath him. He didn't even have a chance to catch a breath before slipping completely under. The goat seemed to take that opportunity to climb right across his chest. Sam could see nothing, but now he himself had to struggle to regain the surface. When he did, he sputtered and gasped for air before he felt Uncle Pete's strong hands grasp him under the arms and drag him backward into the boat. The next thing he knew, he was lying in the bottom of the skiff, looking up at Uncle Pete—and a strangely calm goat.

"I think you're taking this rescue-diver thing a little too far, Sam."

They both laughed at that one while Sam got back up and found his place in the front of the boat—wet and cold now, but all right. He'd even made it back with both his boots still on.

"Wish I had a camera," added Uncle Pete. "I could post it on the Internet for all your friends to see, huh?"

"What friends?" Sam was only half-kidding, but he smiled as he said it. Uncle Pete looked at him kind of sideways.

"Come on. You gotta know how much girls dig guys who put their lives on the line for a goat."

"Oh, no." Sam couldn't help rolling his eyes. "Did you really just say 'dig'?"

"Sorry. All I'm saying is, girls are impressed by this sort of thing, you know. The strong rescuer type. All you've gotta do after this is stand back and let somebody else tell the chicks how good you are, and I know you'll get results sooner or later. Guaranteed."

"Chicks?"

"You know what I mean."

Sam shrugged his shoulders, wondering just a little how Uncle Pete felt qualified to dish out the advice, considering . . .

"I don't know," he replied. "Fishing stupid goats out of a flood doesn't sound too impressive to me."

"That's because you're not looking at it from the girls' perspective. Speaking of which, you probably have your eye on a girl or two who would be totally awestruck if they knew what you were doing. Am I right?"

Sam could feel his cheeks flush a bit as he pretended to straighten out the rope at the front of the boat. Aside from an injured leg that was bleeding onto the floorboards, their goat passenger acted as if he were totally used to boat rides.

"So what's her name?" asked Uncle Pete.

How did he know? Sam wondered. "Uh . . . she doesn't really even know who I am."

"A junior, like you? Cute?"

Sam nodded. "Her name's Arielle."

"Friesen, you mean? Sure! I know who that is. Only, last time I saw her, she was probably in the third grade. Her dad's a sheriff's deputy. In fact, I've been hearing him on the scanner all morning. But watch out for that one. He's got a gun."

"Uncle Pete! She's not in the third grade anymore."

"No doubt. Neither are you."

Uncle Pete chuckled as they headed for shore, toward a sandbag line at the nearest farm. The scanner chirped with the voices of farmers and rescuers—and probably of Deputy Friesen.

"Maybe we don't need to tell Grandma about this?" Sam told Uncle Pete as they jumped out. "I mean, about me falling in the water?"

Uncle Pete laughed once more as he held his radio up to his ear.

"Maybe not. But I think we've rescued all the livestock we can for now. Let's run by the church, see if we can do anything else."

"Uncle Pete—"

But Uncle Pete only turned away as he spoke with someone on the radio.

After returning the goat to its owner's farm, they set out once again across the floodwaters, hurrying back toward the road where they'd first parked their tractor. By now, though, things definitely looked different.

"Water's still rising," Sam called back over his shoulder. He gripped the sides of the boat and tensed his legs as they neared the tractor. Floodwaters now filled many low spots in the pavement and nearly covered the tractor's smaller front wheels.

"Not good," Sam muttered to himself, as they drifted closer.

Chapter
Sixteen

At first Charlotte didn't answer the phone, since she'd gotten used to it being out.

After the fifth ring, though, Emily yelled down the stairs, "Grandma! Are you going to answer that?"

"Oh!" Charlotte reached a hand to her aching back and nearly dropped the knife back into the peanut butter jar. Toby looked up expectantly. "Not now, girl."

The phone rang two more times before she'd finally wiped her fingers and grabbed the receiver off the hook.

The man on the other end of the line introduced himself as Don. She didn't catch his Italian-sounding last name, she was still so flustered.

"I'm sorry, Mister . . ."

"Giordano," he repeated the name more slowly this time before spelling it out for her. "Don Giordano. I'm the state coordinator for the Farm Family of the Year Foundation? Ms. Gauge gave me your name."

"Oh yes, of course. Julie Gauge. I was told you would contact us. But you'll have to excuse me. What is it, Wednesday morning? You're actually the first call we've had in several days, since the phones went down."

"Well then, I'm honored."

Which seemed like an odd thing to say, but oh well.

"Our power is still out though," she explained.

"Yes, I was wondering, since I heard on the evening news that several thousand people in your part of the state are still without power and that you've even had some minor flooding. You're all right then?"

"Oh yes, we're fine. I think I even see some clearing out there."

"And you weren't affected by the floods?"

"Our home is on a bit of a rise, so the flood didn't directly affect us. Several of our neighbors, however, weren't quite as fortunate. I'm not sure I'd call it *minor* flooding, especially not from their perspective."

"I'm very sorry to hear that. Actually, though, Mrs. Stevenson, let me tell you why I'm calling: I wanted to confirm that you're still in a position to host your Farm Family of the Year open house later this month. Because if you're not, well, I have to be honest—that would not be welcome news, even though we could . . . *understand.*"

Charlotte paused for a moment. She didn't like the way he hedged on that last word.

"Mrs. Stevenson?"

"Yes. Yes. I'm sorry. We've just been so focused on the flood."

"But the rain has stopped, right? That's what the Weather Channel said."

"For now. But we don't get your Weather Channel here, even with the power on. And we're just not certain if the rain intends to start again."

"I see. But you're dry for now; that's good news."

Mr. Giordano seemed not to hear what she was saying, so she tried to explain it another way.

"Actually, a neighbor family is staying with us for a few days because the main floor of their house flooded. My son and grandson are out in a little boat, I think, trying to see if they can rescue stranded animals. And my husband is outside, sawing up tree limbs from all the branches that fell."

"That's what I love about you people. You're so resilient. Nothing gets you down. Floods one day, open houses the next. So it sounds as if things are on the mend, and we'll be right on track for the twenty-third."

"Uh . . . Uh . . ." Charlotte stuttered.

"Well, I can't tell you how much I appreciate your flexibility, Mrs. Stevenson."

How could she tell him no when she'd already given her word that they would host the event? On the other hand, with everything that had happened here in the past week, how could she tell him yes? A part of her desperately wished she had never gotten herself into this mess. Couldn't she just have Bob get on the phone and talk to him, telling him to forget the whole thing?

"Actually," she told him, "my husband didn't think—"

"Don't you worry, Mrs. Stevenson," he went on. Hearing him, she imagined that during this man's free time he might make a good used-car salesman. "I'll give you my direct cell number, and if you need anything between now and the big day, don't you hesitate for a moment to call me. Call me anytime. We coordinate these events all over the state this time of year, and our job is to make sure each one is a success."

"That's wonderful, Mr. Giordano, but—"

"So do you have any other questions? I assume you've received the preparation checklist in the mail by now."

"Actually, no."

"Well, it should arrive any day now. It's just to help you know what's expected for the big event. We'll talk again soon?"

When Mr. Giordano hung up, he left Charlotte holding her forehead, wondering how she had let the conversation go so far astray and how he could think their open house would be anything but a flooded disaster area. If he only knew.

Emily peeked around the corner. "Who was that, Grandma?"

Charlotte straightened and turned around before hanging up the receiver and clearing her throat.

"Oh, just the Farm Family of the Year man, checking on us. I believe he called all the way from Lincoln."

"Did you tell him we're flooded out and we can't do it?"

"Well, um . . . he had heard about some of the flooding, yes."

"So they're not going to do it."

Charlotte didn't quite know how to answer.

"What? Grandma! You're kidding, right? I can still see water on the road out there. And you told him we're going to have the open house anyway? Everybody would have to come in a boat."

"That sounds pretty cool," Christopher chimed in as he came up behind his sister and patted Toby. "They could tie up to the back porch. It could be just like that place in San Diego, where all the sailboats tied up to the docks. You know, where Mom used to take us for walks? I always liked that place, especially when we brought bread to feed the seagulls."

"That's dumb, Christopher." Emily crossed her arms the way she did when her little brother annoyed her. "First of all, nobody's going to come in a boat. I was just kidding. And second of all, there aren't any seagulls in Nebraska. Do you know how far we are from the ocean?"

Christopher looked at his grandmother to see if it might be so.

"Your sister's right. We don't get too many seagulls here, although a few years ago I actually did see a couple of lost gulls. There was a pair that followed your grandfather's tractor nearly the entire spring planting season, picking out insects behind his plow. Remember that, Hannah?"

Hannah was just coming down the stairs, drying her hair in a bath towel.

"I remember," she told them. "It was this time of year, actually, only without all the rain. Reminds me of that old Hitchcock movie. Some of the farmers thought it was a sign of good luck."

"Was it?" wondered Christopher.

Charlotte smiled. "It was fun to see them here, Christopher. But only God makes luck, if you can call it that. Does that make sense?"

"Not really."

Emily squinted at her as if she were making the whole thing up, and Charlotte didn't blame her.

When she thought about it a little more, she decided maybe this Mr. Giordano was right. Maybe they would be able to bounce back from this, and sooner than anyone expected. In fact, holding the open house as planned might even boost people's spirits and give them something to look forward to.

Really, what was the harm in trying? Bob was just being his old pessimistic self when he said they shouldn't even try.

But that's when the phone started ringing again, a flood of calls that seemed to have been bottled up during the past forty-eight hours. First it was the insurance company, checking to see what kind of damage they had sustained and promising a quick response from their adjuster. Charlotte tried to pass along as much information about surrounding farms as she could, especially about Hannah and Frank's place.

Seconds after she hung up from the insurance agent, her sister-in-law Rosemary called to make sure they were all right. After assuring her that they were and that everything would surely return to normal soon, Charlotte hung up. But a second later the phone rang again.

"I'll get it," said Emily, picking up the receiver. "It's probably one of my friends, wondering if I'm still alive."

It wasn't, and she handed the phone back to Charlotte with a frown.

"It's Ashley's mom."

This time Charlotte's friend Melody wanted to know if they'd heard of the relief kitchen set up in the Bedford Community Church parking lot. She said if there was any way to get through the roads, they could use a few more volunteers. Apparently several farms from around the county had been affected by the floods, not just here on this stretch of Heather Creek.

"Actually," said Charlotte, "we do have Hannah and Frank Carter staying here overnight. Hannah's right here. Their house . . ."

She explained what had happened to the Carter home and how Bob and Frank wanted to go back today to see if the floodwaters had peaked but that she was worried it still might be too dangerous. Melody replied that she'd heard several roads were inundated, which they already knew. Speaking of which . . .

Charlotte wrinkled her eyebrows in surprise.

"Say that again?" she told Melody. "You heard *what* on the scanner?"

By this time Emily and Christopher were hovering close by, trying to hear what was going on as well.

"I said, my Russ thought he heard Pete on the scanner saying they're having a tough time making it to town through all the water. Even on his tractor."

Charlotte closed her eyes and tried not to imagine the trouble Pete and Sam must have encountered. Now it was more than just stranded livestock.

⌣ Chapter
Seventeen

Nearly an hour later Sam and Uncle Pete finally pulled into the parking lot of the Bedford Community Church, which thankfully looked high and dry. The parking lot had filled with trucks and rescue vehicles. Red and blue emergency lights blinked from behind a cluster of official-looking trucks. Sam scanned the crowd and whistled.

"County sheriff, emergency response team, EMT . . . Man, you'd think there was some kind of disaster going on."

A sheriff's deputy in a tan uniform waved when he noticed them coming. Maybe he was the one Uncle Pete had been talking to on the radio. Uncle Pete pulled in as close as he could and shut down the tractor while the deputy gave them a hand and pointed them to the church basement.

"All in a day's work, huh?" He rested his hands on his hips. "You guys look like you could use something hot to drink. Or maybe something to eat. There's plenty inside."

When he motioned for them to follow, Sam finally caught a glimpse of the man's nametag: Friesen. Of course.

Inside, the church basement had been hurriedly turned into a full-scale rescue center with several rows of cots along one wall, where the senior Sunday school class usually met. Closer to the entry, a couple of folding tables had been set up with piles of blankets, clothes, bars of soap, toothbrushes, and other essentials. In the kitchen, behind the large pass-through window and a portrait of Jesus, a dozen women scurried about, making sandwiches and (by the smell of things) soup and chili. Uncle Pete pointed his nose toward the kitchen and sniffed. He must have noticed that Dana Simons was helping out behind the chow line as well.

"All of a sudden that smells awfully good, huh?"

Sam couldn't agree more, but he nearly tripped over his feet when he saw who else was ladling out relief to the half-dozen farmers in the lunch lineup.

Arielle Friesen.

"Something wrong?" asked Uncle Pete. He noticed too many things, certainly more than Sam wished he would notice. But Sam gamely ordered his noodle legs to walk as Deputy Friesen came up from behind and guided them to the line.

"Be sure and give these boys a nice, big serving, Arielle," the deputy told her in a booming voice that everyone in the room could probably hear. "They just rescued half the county's sheep in their little aluminum boat. Risked their lives, is what I hear."

"Now, hold on," said Uncle Pete as Miss Simons smiled at him. "Wasn't anywhere near that serious."

But Deputy Friesen brushed aside the attempt at modesty, pointing to another deputy at one of the processing tables.

"Barry over there says he heard young Sam and his uncle

plucked a whole flock of animals out of the flood just in time."

"You did?" Arielle raised her eyebrows and smiled at them as she dipped into the chili. "That's really cool!"

"Wasn't so hard." Sam couldn't think of anything that didn't make it sound as if he was bragging. "They're not too smart. Except they do get a little heavy when they're wet."

Luckily the deputy left it at that. "Well," he said with a slap to Sam's back, "I'm sure we'll get all the details later. Right now you boys get something to eat."

Sam's stomach growled just then, another reminder that they'd been up since early morning without a meal. By this time, Grandma was probably getting pretty worried, note or no note. Meanwhile, Arielle served him an extra scoop and seemed to hide a shy smile of her own as she did. Or maybe Sam was just imagining it.

"So you drafted Arielle into service?" Uncle Pete asked the deputy.

"The hazards of being a deputy's daughter." Deputy Friesen waved his hand toward Arielle, who had tied her raven-black hair in a ponytail. "Though I have to say, she actually volunteered as soon as we started setting up this morning, didn't you, Ari?"

"Had to do something, Dad." She shook her head. "With no school today."

"That's right," replied the deputy. "Keep you out of trouble. Hey, but you two are in the same grade, aren't you?"

Sam and Arielle both nodded their yes, and Sam had to look away when she caught his eye. She stood only a couple of inches shorter than Sam, and to him looked like a runner—or a model—but not the kind who wore a lot of goopy makeup, and way different from most of the girls he'd known back in San Diego. He didn't think they would volunteer their days off ladling chili and serving cornbread to a bunch of hungry, dirty farmers and flood survivors.

She scooped them up an extra piece of cornbread with her plastic-gloved hand, but once more Sam felt his throat go dry as he tried to think of something intelligent to say. Well, here was his chance, right? He did everything possible not to stare, or drop his tray, or do something stupid.

"Thanks," he finally managed, looking up from studying his chili long enough to prove he wasn't a complete nerd.

Thanks? That was the best he could come up with?

Even so, Arielle did have a terrific smile—pretty as anything, with bright white teeth lined up in two nice rows, but with something extra too. Sparkling dark blue eyes, for instance, and an easy laugh. He'd noticed that she laughed a lot when she was around her friends.

Surely someone with that nice of a smile would have tons of guys already asking her out to the junior prom next month, he thought. But for a delicious couple of seconds he allowed himself a wild and crazy thought.

He pictured himself in one of those fancy prom jackets, Arielle on his arm and wearing the twenty-five-dollar orchid corsage he'd picked out for her at Filly's Flower Shop. He'd be extra-careful not to step on her toes when they were dancing—something he could hardly imagine himself doing but she was probably really good at. She would be wearing some of that cool perfume he would be able to smell when his face was about three inches from hers, and the thought made his heart race even now. *No, no, no!* He scolded himself for even imagining the impossible prom scene. After all, he thought, she probably already had a steady boyfriend, even if Sam didn't know about it. She had to.

Probably some guy she's gone to school with since she was five years old, he thought. *A senior who drives a shiny new black pickup truck and wears a big shiny belt buckle that he won at the fair for roping calves. And his parents are probably best friends with her parents . . .*

Sam didn't imagine his goat-roping experience during the flood would go far to raise his standing. Nobody received a big belt buckle or a blue ribbon for being a doofus and falling in the water.

The good news was that Arielle didn't seem to have a guy with an arm around her shoulder. Mainly she hung around with mixed groups of choir and drama people at school, as far as he could tell.

The bad news was that Sam had no idea how to break through the group. It was like she was surrounded by the Secret Service. He could just imagine the scene if he ever tried.

Uncle Pete nudged him out of his fatalistic daydream as they carried their meal to a folding table and sat down. Fortunately, Sam's imaginary calf roper with the big belt buckle was nowhere to be found.

"What did I tell you?" Uncle Pete told him, but not loud enough for anyone else to hear. "She digs it."

Uncle Pete just didn't get it. Sam groaned, and he hoped his red cheeks wouldn't look too obvious from across the room.

Chapter Eighteen

Charlotte didn't mind having more people for dinner again on Friday. Not in the least. In fact, if it weren't for the circumstances, the flood, and the mounting pressure from what she had to do to prepare for the upcoming open house, having Hannah and Frank stay with them might be a treat.

"It's good that you're here," she told Hannah as they cleared away the empty plates. No leftovers tonight. "I mean, not good that you *have* to be. Oh, dear. You know what I mean."

Now she'd done it. She bit her lip.

Hannah shook her head and smiled as she ferried a load of dishes to the kitchen counter. "Sure I know what you mean. Heavens, we're just so grateful for everything you've done to make us welcome, Charlotte. Especially considering everything on your plate right now!"

She traded glances with Frank, still seated at the far end of the table, next to Bob. They seemed to be planning something, probably discussing more details for restoring Hannah and Frank's home.

"Yeah, we're supposed to meet with the contractor and some of the cleanup crew tomorrow again," said Frank, straightening up and pushing back his chair with a squeak. "Didn't look so good today."

"But they're going to fix your house, aren't they?" Christopher wanted to know as he speared his last green bean.

"Sure they are," answered Pete. But Frank still looked as if he had more to say.

"Actually, uh, we've decided we're going to be staying with my sister in town, starting tomorrow. Ruth has an extra bedroom."

"Oh." Charlotte wasn't sure why Frank looked at the floor while Hannah busied herself filling the sink with hot water and suds. "But you know you're always welcome to stay here as long as you like, don't you?"

This time Hannah was letting Frank do all the talking. "Sure we do," he said. "And you know how much we appreciate your open door here. Really we do. It's just, you know, Ruth really wanted us to stay there. And it's just for a few days, until we get the place cleaned back up."

Perhaps that was optimistic, given the extent of the flood damage at the Carter farm. But Charlotte wasn't going to mention the fact that here they lived just down the road while Frank's sister lived all the way in town. Or that Ruth owned a very modest two-bedroom cottage, hardly enough room for three adults, and here they had extra bedrooms. No. Hannah and Frank should do what was best for their family.

Charlotte put on her best smile. "You kids do what you have to do," she said. "And just tell us whenever you need something."

"Kids?" asked Christopher. "I thought *we* were the kids."

"It's just an expression, silly," said his big sister, saving Charlotte the trouble. By that time they had cleared off the rest of the table and Emily had brought out a fresh-baked cherry cobbler, which clearly got her Uncle Pete's attention.

"Ah, I was wondering what smelled so good," he said, taking up his fork and holding it at the ready. "Did you bake that, Emily, or did Grandma?"

"What do you think?" Emily smiled back, and it warmed Charlotte's heart to realize her granddaughter could prepare a nice dessert like that now, only asking for directions once or twice.

"Save some for me!" said Christopher as Emily scooped the cobbler into bowls and passed it around. Charlotte had a pretty good idea she would not have to put away any leftovers from dessert either. Just as well. She was about to reach for the coffeepot and pour each of the adults a cup when the phone rang.

"I'll get it!" said Emily, but her hands were still full, serving up cobbler.

"No, you stay right there." Charlotte waved her off, handed the coffeepot to Bob, and picked up the kitchen receiver herself. "Hello?"

"Oh, Mrs. Stevenson, I'm so glad it's you! Is Emily close by?"

Charlotte recognized the voice of Ashley Givens, Emily's best friend. Even so, she had to plug her free ear to hear over the kitchen noise and the laughing. Pete was telling another of his jokes.

"Why, yes," she replied. "I'll get—"

"No, no, no! Please!" Ashley interrupted. "I meant, is she close by where she can hear what you're saying?"

"Well, as a matter of fact, yes."

This all sounded a little too mysterious. What was Ashley getting at?

"Okay. Then all you have to do is pretend you're talking to some other adult. Like I'm someone from church."

"Pardon me?"

"Look, I know this sounds kind of strange, Mrs. Stevenson, but I didn't know how else to ask you except to call."

That's when Charlotte noticed Hannah and Frank politely setting their dishes of cobbler aside, apparently waiting for Charlotte to finish her conversation.

"Please, you two," she told them, "don't wait."

"Huh?" Ashley obviously thought Charlotte was talking to her.

"Oh, I'm sorry." Charlotte returned to the phone. "I was . . . never mind. What were you saying?"

Back on track, Ashley launched right back into her story. "Okay. So tomorrow . . . that's Saturday, right? I'm calling because we sort of need your help."

"We?"

"Me and Megan and Rachel. We would have told you before. In fact, Megan was supposed to talk to you at church last week, after Sunday school? But it turns out she was sick with a really, really bad migraine and she had to stay home that day, like with the shades drawn and the TV turned way down low. But Megan gets those migraines all the time, and she has to take these really nasty pills that make her feel sick to her stomach? I feel bad for her."

"I hope she's doing better."

"Oh, totally. Now she runs every day."

Well, that was good. But by this time Emily gave her grandmother a curious look and mouthed the words, "Who's that?"

Charlotte didn't answer. Instead she shook her head and turned her back to the kitchen while stretching the phone cord.

"So then . . ." Charlotte lowered her voice even more, feeling downright conspiratorial. "What did you have in mind?"

"Well, we didn't want to ruin your plans. You were going to make a birthday dinner for her, right?"

"Well, yes, I was still thinking along those lines." *Or something like that.*

Ashley went on. "Okay, so here's the thing: We've been wanting to have this surprise birthday party for Emily for like the longest time. And now we think we have it figured out, if it's okay with you. We just need someone to get her to the Bedford Bowl tomorrow night."

"And you'd like me to do that."

"Mr. Stevenson could come too. I mean, if he wants. Unless he's too busy. But I checked, and there's no leagues going on tomorrow night."

"That would be a problem, I suppose."

"Yeah. So Emily just can't know where she's going, and she can't know we're all going to be waiting for her there. What do you think?"

"Of course." Charlotte chose her words carefully, doing her best not to give anything away from her side of the conversation. "What time did you have in mind?"

"We thought about six? We'll have pizza and cake and

stuff. You won't have to bring anything, unless you want to."

A slight change of plans, to put it mildly.

Stay flexible, Charlotte reminded herself, taking a deep breath. *If her friends want to do this for her, well, that's very sweet of them. Even on this short notice.*

But Charlotte wondered as she peeked back over her shoulder at her family and the Carters, who were both finishing their desserts. How was she going to keep from feeding Emily tomorrow night without explaining the entire plan?

"So you'll do it?" Ashley sounded hopeful on the other end of the line. "It's okay if we change plans like this?"

By this time Bob and Pete had started to push their chairs back from the table, stretching their arms as if ready to stand up. Frank and Hannah spoke quietly with each other. Christopher had crawled under the table to pester the cat while Sam sat in his own little world, scraping his dessert plate and licking his fork. Emily, meanwhile, kept a curious eye turned in Charlotte's direction.

"Of course it's okay, dear." Charlotte had to stay upbeat. "It's just that, well, you know . . ."

She paused, giving Ashley a chance to figure out her dilemma.

"Mrs. Stevenson? Is Emily still listening?"

"That's right."

"Oh! So I'll bet she's going to be wondering what's going on, huh?"

"Exactly."

"Well, hmm. I know! You don't need to lie. Just don't tell her the truth. I mean, you know what I mean."

"I'm not sure I do. But I suppose we'll think of something."

"Fantastic! I knew you'd come through! Thanks, Mrs. Stevenson."

Charlotte still wasn't sure what to say as she hung up the phone, though she fully expected Emily's curious "Who was that, Grandma?"

"That was..." She scratched her head and cleared her throat, stalling. Just then the phone graciously rang once again.

"Why don't you get it this time?" she told Emily. "It's probably for you."

Maybe yes, and maybe no. But before anyone could ask anything else, she hurried to the sink to finish her dishes and add to her mental to-do list.

Chapter Nineteen

The next morning—Saturday—Charlotte stepped gingerly out of her car, shading her eyes against the morning sun to see what was left of the Carter farm. As her feet sank in the mud, she recalled Hannah's warning to be prepared for the worst. Well, all right then—she was.

At the same time, she took a deep breath and prepared for her job as cheerleader, ignoring the nagging ache in her lower back. The ibuprofen she'd taken that morning had deadened the pain a bit, though not nearly enough to keep her from wincing. Too bad ibuprofen couldn't cure what had just happened to Hannah's home.

Oh, Hannah. Her heart fell as she paused to take it all in. Dirty leaves and branches covered the back yard, but that wasn't nearly the worst of it. Floodwaters had brought with them nearly every foul thing one could imagine—and many unimaginable things, besides. The late morning sun, though welcome as it peeked through the clouds, brought to light a witch's brew of garbage and filth strewn all over the property in the wake of the still-receding waters. The sight nearly made her cry while the stench turned her stomach. Something had very obviously died here—and Charlotte hoped it wasn't Hannah and Frank's hope.

Even the farmer's wife—well accustomed to barnyard aromas—could not stomach this flood's unexpected aftermath. Charlotte held a hand over her face, afraid to even breathe. She only remembered her duty to encourage Hannah as her friend stepped out onto the front porch through the opening where the front door used to hang. Perhaps it had been taken off its hinges on purpose.

"There you are!" Hannah greeted her with a wave and a song in her voice that really should not have been there. "I thought I heard your car."

The dust mask on Hannah's face prevented Charlotte from seeing her friend's true expression, so she focused on her eyes. They seemed the same—bright and easygoing, full of warmth. For her part, however, Hannah would not be able to miss Charlotte's shock.

"Yeah, that's what I thought too," said Hannah, pulling off her mask and stepping gingerly down the silt-covered front steps to greet her. She did not touch the railings, covered in slime as they were. "I already cried all morning. Trust me; it's a mess."

Actually, it was much more than that.

Inside, Frank and two other men mucked out the rooms as they would a filthy barn floor, sending muddy waves out the front and back doors with their snow shovels and push brooms. Beyond Frank himself, Charlotte couldn't quite tell who hid behind the masks and hoods, but they pushed through without heed to the women.

Though Charlotte knew the sandbagging teams had

cleared out much of the light furniture before the worst of the flood hit, they apparently hadn't been able to rescue everything. Bottles, cans, and shredded paper now lay everywhere, scattered in the most unlikely spots. A bottle of shampoo had landed right-side up on the cushion of a sofa that, because of its size, had been left behind in the panic. Charlotte thought it had been cream with white and blue flowers before; now, like everything else, it had taken on the color of coffee with a touch of cream. The ruined piece of furniture would now be hauled off to the dump, and soon, please.

Elsewhere a pile of mud-encrusted drapes lay crumpled in the corner next to a heavy oak buffet that had also been too heavy to move. Hannah stooped to open the buffet's lower cabinet, where she stored china. She pulled out one of her best Blue Willow dishes, now coated like everything else with the flood's disagreeable brown ooze.

Hannah set the plate down and drew her finger across the cabinet door, leaving a trail in the grime.

"You know, this belonged to Frank's grandmother," she said, her lip now trembling. She would only be able to keep up the sunny expression for so long.

"We'll clean it up again," Charlotte told her, not really knowing for certain if the antique would stand up any better to cleaning than it had to the flood. Already the cabinet door appeared to have warped; it refused to close. Hannah probably knew the truth as well.

"I'm so sorry" was all Charlotte could say. She shuddered to think what her house would look like in this kind of state, but she was actually afraid to thank God for being spared. In the face of Hannah's loss, somehow it didn't seem right.

"So am I." Hannah pointed to a greasy brown line running across her kitchen wall, just below the level of her kitchen countertops. "See there? It took out everything, got into the ductwork and the walls, the plug-ins, everything. We tried to rescue as much stuff as we could, and maybe insurance will cover some. But right now it doesn't look as if . . ."

She didn't need to finish. Her tears returned as the women stood arm-in-arm in Hannah's kitchen and stared quietly at the devastation. It was one thing, thought Charlotte, to see flooding on the television. She still vividly remembered the pity she'd felt seeing hurricane victims on the evening news and hearing of all the flood damage in Florida and on the Gulf Coast. At the time, she and Bob had been moved to contribute both to the Red Cross and to their church's own relief fund.

But that tragedy had seemed so far off, like Bangladesh or China, and without much effort it could be safely held at arm's length, just like so many other tragedies that flashed into their living room before the channel was changed. In that respect, Bob was usually quick with the remote.

This, on the other hand, was altogether different—a gut-check to assault her senses and a heartbreak whose channel she could not avoid. Her stomach roiled at seeing every corner of Hannah's home violated this way. Mud on the floor, mud in the cupboards, mud everywhere. She wished she had not stepped inside, except for the opportunity to comfort Hannah. At that, however, she feared she had not succeeded.

"Coming through!" yelled one of the men. Hannah and Charlotte stood to the side as he took a pressure hose to the mess in the kitchen. The stench reminded her of dead fish rotting in the sun. She held her nose as she pressed her hand to her face, thinking it ironic that they were using water to try to clean the damage that water had caused.

"I know what you mean," Hannah told her, holding her own nose. "And I thought I was getting used to it."

Frank's other helper had taken to ripping out soggy wallboard, throwing it into a large rolling garbage can. He started in the downstairs bathroom, grunting as he tossed flabby waterlogged pieces across the room.

"I should get out of your way," Charlotte told Hannah.

"No, me too," replied Hannah. "There's not much I can do here right now except slow them down. Maybe I should just go back to see how Ruth is doing."

They moved out the front door once again just as spray from the high-pressure hose splattered mud and debris their way. This would not be an easy or agreeable task. Yet Charlotte caught a glimpse of hope in Hannah's eyes, even as the sun peeked through clouds outside.

"You let me know how I can help," Charlotte told her friend, enveloping her in a hug. It was, as it turned out, as much for her as for Hannah. "We'll get through this."

Charlotte wasn't actually sure she believed her own words, even if Hannah did.

"I know we will," Hannah answered, drying her tears and looking Charlotte in the eyes. "Right now I'm letting Frank and his brothers do the dirty work, but maybe in a few days there'll be something useful we can do. Meanwhile, you let me know if you need any help over at your house too, okay? Remember: I owe you, Charlotte Stevenson."

"You mean for the short time you stayed with us? Please!

You would have done the same for us, I'm sure, had the situation been different."

"Of course we would have. But Charlotte . . ." She rested a hand on Charlotte's shoulder, and her expression went serious. "I don't know if it was just the strain of everyone being there, or the flood, but . . . you and Bob . . . is everything okay between you?"

Charlotte pressed her lips together, and for a moment she couldn't look Hannah in the eye.

"I'm sorry." Hannah cut in before Charlotte could answer. "I really shouldn't have even mentioned it. It's none of my business."

"No, no; it's all right. He's just been working so hard. You know. We're all tired. Under a lot of stress. Sometimes we get a little cranky. I know I do."

Charlotte wasn't quite sure she believed her own explanation. Hannah had seen something—what was it, exactly? But now she did an admirable job of changing the subject to something more cheery.

"I knew that's all it was," she said, "and I'm sorry for even bringing it up. You must be thinking about fixing up for the open house now."

"What?" Charlotte tried to lighten up as well. "You have more than enough on your plate without worrying about my open house, girl."

She thought of the plate Hannah had pulled out of her buffet and regretted the unfortunate choice of words. Hannah didn't seem to notice.

"No, I'm serious, Charlotte. This is bigger than what I can handle, just like the open house is bigger than what you can handle. We need to help each other."

"Of course we do." Charlotte nodded her head, not mentioning what Bob had said about canceling the event. But Hannah's words did remind her of the phone call she really needed to make to Julie Gauge at the Farm Family of the Year office. In light of all this devastation, she knew she couldn't ask Hannah—or any of her other neighbors—to help with the open house. Not now. Not with all this flood damage around them. How could she?

"And what about your back?" asked Hannah. "Here I am, so worried about myself that I completely forgot how you'd hurt yourself."

"Hurt myself? Come on. I'm taking aspirin for it. Ibuprofen. You know."

"And it's working? Come on, honestly?"

"Well . . ."

"You should let me take you in to see Dr. Carr. He—"

"Hannah." Charlotte interrupted her. "I appreciate your concern. But really, we have a lot of other things to do besides going in to see the doctor for a silly backache."

"That's just it though, Charlotte. I think it's more than just a silly backache. I've seen the way you're in pain, and there's nothing silly about that. I think you need to do something about it, and now."

Charlotte wagged a finger at her in mock seriousness. "Thank you, Hannah. I appreciate your concern; I really do. But you let me be the judge of how silly the pain is—or if it's even a pain, at all. And now I need to get home. After all, Emily's birthday party is tonight."

By the time she returned home, however, she could hardly get through all the pickups parked between her house and the barn—perhaps as many as fifteen or sixteen.

Bill's silver Toyota looked conspicuous in the middle of the workaday pickups, almost as conspicuous as he did himself, standing in the middle of the farmers. Never mind that he had grown up on this place.

Pete stood on a tailgate with his hands raised, trying to get the assembled group's attention. Below him stood Dan Hostetler, whose wife Amanda made some of the best desserts for Bedford Community Church potlucks. Beside Dan stood Hank Richmond, whose wife Janie didn't talk much, and neither did he. Even Dave Meyers was there; his farmhouse had surely been overtaken by floodwaters, the same as the Carters'. Maybe worse. Heather Creek ran right through their place, and Charlotte made a mental note to call his wife DeeDee real soon. Walt Freeman from just down the road was there too.

As Toby bounded up to greet her, Charlotte stood outside her car, listening.

"All I'm trying to say, guys, is that we need to work together to help the families whose places were hit the hardest. If we wait on the government, it'll be next year. No offense, Bill."

Bill held up his hands as if he understood. What could the mayor of River Bend do to help anyway? Several of the men in the crowd murmured their agreement as Pete pointed to Dave Meyers.

"Dave, how are your fields looking?"

"Still mostly underwater." Dave removed his John Deere cap and scratched his bald dome. "It's clearing, but slower'n I'd like."

Now Bob spoke up from where he stood next to his son. "We just gotta be careful not to be plowing in the mud, before it dries out. I don't have to tell you it doesn't do any good to be planting before it's ready."

"I hear what you're saying, Bob." Dan Hostetler piped up. "But if we wait too long, that's almost as bad. Either way, we're in a tough spot. The fields aren't going to plant themselves, you know."

"Okay, that's why we're here." Pete went on, and the clear authority in his voice surprised even his mother. Was this the same Pete? "We'll share equipment and labor whenever we can. So as soon as Dave's fields dry out, for instance, as many of us as can, will come blitz the planting. We'll get it done quicker that way, because every day counts. Me and Dad, we're going to be coordinating here out of Heather Creek Farm. Let us know what you can do and when you need help. And we pray for sunny weather. Any questions?"

"Yeah." Dan raised his hand. "My wife wants to know what kind of food she's supposed to bring to the open house. It's still on, isn't it?"

Some of the guys chuckled, and certainly the question sounded a little strange—especially coming from Dan. Bob didn't disguise his frown but remained silent as everyone turned to see what Charlotte would say. So they had noticed her arrive, after all.

"Mom?" asked Pete.

"Ah, well . . ." Caught off guard, Charlotte fumbled for words but raised her voice so they could hear her. Her eyes met Bob's for just a moment before he looked away. What to say?

"You just tell Amanda I'll be getting ahold of her real soon."

Well, that seemed to satisfy the men, as Charlotte imagined preparing for the Farm Family of the Year open house was probably the last thing on their minds—as it had been on hers.

She retreated to her kitchen but kept an eye on the men through the window as they discussed their planting schedules. From the look of things, they all had plenty of questions. How could they not? She'd never seen them work together quite like this.

When the phone rang, she took a message for Pete from Bud Smithgall, three miles down the road and apparently not hit so badly by the flood. He said he was willing to help with the planting of any fields that needed help. She thanked him and scribbled his name on the pad next to the phone, noting the lengthy to-do list she'd written there earlier that day.

She paused a moment, remembering what Hannah had said about helping each other. Outside her back door, a dozen crusty farmers with mud on their boots were talking about how to share their equipment and get the daunting task of spring planting accomplished—despite what had just hit them.

She sighed, hoping that by going ahead with the open house she would not put more of a wedge between her and her husband than there already was. But he would see. And surely he would understand—if not right away, then eventually.

All right then. No more waffling. She vigorously struck out the line that read, "Call to cancel open house."

⌣ Chapter Twenty

Charlotte's original to-do-for-the-open-house list grew from ten items to at least thirty or more, and that's when she quit counting. With less than a week to go before the April 23 target, she thought it better not to know just how impossible it would be.

Still, she couldn't help scanning the list just once more as she stood in the middle of the little produce department at Herko's Grocery just after lunchtime on Saturday. Each to-do reminded her of one more thing to buy, and if Bob saw how far beyond their grocery budget they were this month . . . Well, she would worry about that later. Right now, she was trying to remember if she had enough relish at home for the potato salad she would make, or if she should pick up another couple of jars while she was here.

Everything on her list reminded her of something else—and not just groceries. She went down the list again . . .

Pick up flood debris in the yard. Check. They would need another package of garbage bags.

Fix picnic tables behind barn. Perhaps she'd need another couple of plastic tablecloths. No, three.

Borrow punch bowls. Besides lemonade mix, they would also need plenty of coffee. Maybe she could use one or two more coffeemakers from the church. Oh, and folding tables.

Repaint the barn, although it was still too wet.

Fix two broken park benches.

Cut and trim lawn. Prune bushes. Secure loose step on back porch. Replace cracked window. Replace lettering on mailbox. Get rid of burn pile. Paint . . .

The list went on, down the page and beyond. Only a week left? Not to mention the birthday cake and candles she needed for Emily's birthday celebration that night. Nothing like waiting until the last moment!

"Looks like quite a lot of groceries to get there." DeeDee Meyers interrupted Charlotte's worrying as the little woman rolled by with her cart.

"Oh, DeeDee!" Charlotte stuffed her list back into her purse. "I didn't see you coming."

"Lost in thought, eh? I don't blame you." DeeDee smiled, though her round face seemed wrinkled in its own worry. Her makeup seemed a little smeared as well, and she looked as if she'd been crying. "Dave told me you're still planning on the Farm Family open house, no matter what. I say that's good. Go for it."

"Well, don't tell anyone, but I'm not so sure."

"No? Why not?"

"For one thing, I have no idea how many to expect. So I have no idea how many napkins to buy, or how much lemonade to mix, or how much it's all going to cost. Or even if I can get it all done in time. You should see the list of things I need to get done."

DeeDee nodded, but with a far-off look in her eyes as she glanced toward the windows at the front of the little grocery.

When Charlotte remembered, she could have pinched herself. "Oh, I'm sorry, DeeDee. Here I am prattling on about my troubles, when I totally forgot to ask about your house. How are you and Dave managing?"

DeeDee turned back with a brave face, but Charlotte could tell right away that it only covered something else.

"We're doing great," she told Charlotte, her voice wavering just a bit. "I told Dave we can just pretend we're camping at Crystal Lake, with all the water in our back yard. But the good news is, it's going away fast!"

Now she was obviously trying too hard to sound cheerful. Charlotte had to ask though.

"Your house?" She remembered the small but immaculate farmhouse Dave and DeeDee had completely remodeled a couple of years ago. DeeDee swallowed hard.

"Dave says we fixed it up once, so we can do it again. Good thing it's not so cold, so we're nice and cozy in our travel trailer."

Another homeless family, then. But DeeDee went on as if they were discussing a new recipe.

"Actually, Dave and some of the other men are getting together to help each other stay on track, get the planting done, that sort of thing. Oh, but you already know that! I heard your Pete is really stepping up. You must be very proud of him."

"Pete, yes." Charlotte nodded. News traveled fast. "Of course we are."

There was that word again: *proud*. But without Bob there to add his two cents' worth, Charlotte wasn't quite sure she'd said the right thing. But they *were* proud of Pete, were they not?

"And we're all very excited about the open house." DeeDee patted Charlotte's hand. "I guess it takes more than a little rain to slow down a Nebraska farm family, right?"

The odd part was being on the receiving end of the encouragement, when Charlotte knew it should have been the other way around. After all, whose home had been wiped out? After saying her good-byes, Charlotte decided she'd had enough of her list for the time being and headed for one of the three checkout lanes.

"YOU MEAN YOU CAN'T TAKE just an hour off to celebrate your granddaughter's birthday?" Charlotte tried to keep her voice down as she swirled frosting on the top of Emily's chocolate cake. "You said you would, before. And she's only turning fifteen once, you know."

Bob frowned as he washed his hands in the kitchen sink, something Charlotte had asked him a hundred times to please not do. Please use the bathroom sink, she'd told him. But this time the argument—rather, the *discussion*—was not about leaving a mess in the sink.

"Can't help it. Got some welding I have to take care of if I'm going to get that seeder working again," he told her. "Nobody else is going to do it for me, you know. This party thing just come up all of a sudden? Thought she was just having a couple friends over."

"Ashley Givens called me last night to say what the girls were planning. She was nice enough to ask us to come along."

"Well, sure. But who else was going to drive her? Sam?"

"Sam could drive her. I just thought it would be nice if we did."

"Sounds like more than an hour to me."

This was going from bad to worse.

"So now you're worried about a few minutes? Bob, I know it's been crazy this past couple of weeks. But you said you would be here for the dinner tonight. Before you know it, Emily's going to be grown and gone, and you know how that feels."

"I can't predict when something breaks. And don't start comparing her to Denise."

"I'm not comparing her to Denise. All I'm saying is, three or four more years will pass so quickly, and then—"

"And then none of us will be here if I don't get this seeder fixed. Feel free to go if you want, but I really have to get this done."

Charlotte held a finger to her lips at the sound of feet coming down the stairs. A moment later Emily poked her head around the corner, and Charlotte couldn't be sure if the puzzled look on her granddaughter's face meant that she had overheard or not.

"When's dinner, Grandma?" She glanced from the kitchen clock to the cake Charlotte quickly held behind her back. By 5:20 Charlotte would usually have something simmering on the stove or warming in the oven. "Ashley's supposed to be coming over pretty soon."

Charlotte looked at her stubborn husband one last time, but he only grabbed a clean dishtowel to wipe the rest of the dirt off his hands. Another pet peeve . . .

"Actually, my dear birthday girl," said Charlotte, "we're having a sort of girls' night out. You and me, and . . . well, I'm not disclosing any details. I've spoken with Ashley. But we're leaving in ten minutes."

"What?" Emily obviously didn't get it. "You talked to Ashley? What's going on? Where are we going?"

"Too many questions. We're leaving in . . ." Charlotte checked the clock again. "Eight minutes."

"But what about Grandpa and the boys?"

By this time Bob was rummaging around in the pantry.

"Me? I'm just heatin' up a can of beans over the tractor radiator for the boys and me. Ever had beans like that? Beats a restaurant."

"Eeeeuuw, cooking on a tractor?" Emily wrinkled her nose. "I like beans, but you're just being silly, Grandpa."

He came out of the pantry with a can of beans in each hand.

"Aren't you?" Now Emily didn't sound so sure.

If that's the way Bob was going to be, Charlotte would let him take care of dinner for once. It was his choice. She set the cake down on the counter, and then left to change her clothes and fix her hair.

Chapter
Twenty-One

Was Emily really that deep in thought, or just wondering what was going on? In any case, Charlotte grew tired of asking questions that only resulted in one-word answers.

School was *fine*. Her teachers were *okay*. And *no*, none of her friends minded the two days they missed because of the floods.

I need to learn how to ask questions she can't just answer with one word, thought Charlotte. But interviewing had never been her best skill. And as they reached the backside of Bedford's Lincoln Street stores, she wondered if perhaps it had been a mistake to drive Emily in by herself. What was she going to do while the girls were enjoying themselves anyway?

On the other hand, Ashley had invited her, hadn't she? Perhaps Emily's friends wouldn't mind Charlotte lingering in the background.

"You sure you can't say where we're going?" asked Emily. Surely she had it figured out by now. "Are we going to Mel's Place?"

"You'll find out." Charlotte had to admit by now that she was beginning to enjoy this surprise. In fact, she could almost imagine herself at fifteen or sixteen again, riding with Becky Thompson in Becky's father's truck. She and Becky would drive up and down Lincoln Street on Saturday nights in July when they had finished all their chores and had nothing better to do.

She checked her watch and circled the block again, just to be sure they were giving Ashley and the others enough time. She pointed out a storefront, the place Arleta's Cut 'n' Curl now occupied.

"That's where the Imperial used to be, you know. We got to see all the new films when my father was the manager there."

"Uh-huh." Emily nodded. Perhaps she'd heard this story before. No matter.

"I used to love Tony Randall," Charlotte went on as they circled the block once more. Emily was probably really wondering by now. "Becky and I saw *Spartacus*, with Kirk Douglas, three times, I think."

Of course, that was only a couple of years before the Bedford Bowl was built. Now Emily actually started to giggle as they finally pulled into the parking lot.

"What's so funny?" asked Charlotte.

"Bowling?" Emily nearly snorted. "You're actually taking me bowling?"

"Well, why not?"

"But . . . what about your back? I don't want you to get hurt again."

"My back, I'll have you know, is just fine. Come to think of it, I didn't even have to take any ibuprofen this morning. It might even be good for it to stretch out a little."

"I don't know if it's a good idea for you." Emily still didn't move to get out of the car, though Charlotte had already set the brake. "You're serious?"

"Absolutely. Now come on."

Charlotte's watch said ten after six. The extra few minutes should have given Ashley and her friends plenty of time to get here ahead of them to prepare whatever it was they were going to prepare.

"I don't know, Grandma. I always thought these kinds of places were kind of smoky and sleazy."

"The Bedford Bowl? I don't think—"

When Charlotte held open the glass front door, they were greeted by an avalanche of sound: bowling balls exploding into the back wall, video games buzzing and beeping, a country station blaring, and plenty of laughter. Charlotte sniffed the air before stepping inside. Good. Just pizza and popcorn, no smoke.

Even so, Emily held back a little until she noticed a cluster of three girls sitting at one of the three lanes. Ashley, Megan, and Rachel. They all turned at some unseen signal and shouted in unison: "Surprise!"

"Wait a minute." Emily looked up at her grandmother with wide eyes. "How did you . . . how did they . . . ?"

Charlotte had to laugh. "Your friends wanted me to bring you here, so I did."

Ashley and the others gathered around. "Come on, Emily." Ashley took her hand and tugged her toward their lane. "The loser has to pay for all the cake and ice cream— kidding!"

Charlotte hung back for a moment, unsure how far her

unfamiliar role as chauffeur and chaperone extended into the Bedford Bowl. Suddenly a voice behind her made her jump.

"Grandma!" Christopher stepped up beside her, along with Sam, Pete and Bob. "Are you going to bowl with us too?"

"What? How did you get here so soon?" She wasn't sure what they had in mind, especially not Bob. "I thought you all had work to do."

"We followed you!" announced Christopher. "Except you were going in circles. We even brought the cake!"

"We decided a little break wouldn't hurt," Bob told her as he slipped off his jacket. "And these guys think they can beat me in bowling."

"But we haven't been bowling in years, Bob. Are you sure you remember how?"

Bob held up a finger, looking assured as he headed for the food counter and the rental shoes. "You watch."

"Besides." Pete smiled at her. "Nobody really wanted to cook, and Dad said he'd pay for a chili dog."

"I didn't say I'd pay for *you*," Bob said over his shoulder.

For the next several minutes they set themselves up with bowling shoes, sodas, and hot dogs. While Christopher searched for the perfect bowling ball, Charlotte and Bob watched the girls start their game in the next lane.

"I'm really glad you changed your mind," Charlotte told Bob. But he kept his eye on their scorecards, licking his pencil and filling in their names.

"Christopher didn't give me any choice," he answered. "When the little guy found out about his sister's party, there was no stopping him. Amazing how fast he can move sometimes."

"Well, I'm still glad you're here."

"Yeah, but listen. I don't know if it's such a good idea that you play. I thought you were just going to come here and watch the girls."

"You let me worry about that." She hefted a child-size orange-and-purple ball with no problem. "It's really not that big, and I've been feeling fine."

"All the same, I don't think you ought to be lifting anything."

Sam came back with his choice of bowling ball just then, looking around with a puzzled expression.

"Where's the scoring machine?" he wondered, looking all around. "This has got to be the lamest bowling alley in the world. Only three lanes. And I *so* can't believe there's no scoring machine."

"You're looking at the scoring machine." Bob poked a thumb at his chest, but Sam only looked all the more dubious.

"You know how to do that?"

"Don't look so surprised. I can add. And I know how to score if you make a strike or a spare. Not that it's going to happen, but—"

"*I* will!" announced Christopher. "I'm going to get twenty strikes, and . . . but, is that good? I don't want to strike out."

"You can't strike out in bowling," Sam told him, "and you can't get twenty strikes. I don't think."

Pete laughed. "You guys can make as many strikes as you want."

"Okay, okay." Sam still didn't look convinced. "But there's no screen for the scores. Every bowling alley I've ever been to had a screen for the scores."

By then the girls were well into their game, and all four of them squealed as Ashley jumped up and down. "I made it past the gutters!" she told them.

Charlotte had no idea how they were keeping score over there, but perhaps that didn't matter very much. Emily seemed to be deep in conversation and pizza, and that was probably all that mattered.

"Your turn, Mom." Pete pointed at the lighted pins in the distance. All right, then. Charlotte gingerly picked up her orange-and-purple ball and hefted it in front of her. So far, so good. She looked around the alley and paused. It had been a few years, after all.

Over in lane one, two young men were doing their best to impress the four girls in lane three, flexing their muscles and swinging their arms as they hurled the ball down the lane. The girls, fortunately, didn't seem to notice.

"That's Dean Wallace," Sam told her, pretending not to look. "He's a jerk."

"Sam!" She started to wind up. "You shouldn't say that about people."

"Only if it's true."

By this time, Charlotte was into her approach: sight the pins, three steps down the lane, swing the ball, and . . .

"Oh no!" she whispered as the ball hit the floor with a loud thump and nearly bounced over into the next lane before settling into the gutter. Worse than that, she clamped her jaw and swallowed back the sudden pain that shot through her back. *Not again!* She took a deep breath and smiled, though, before turning back to the group.

"Guess it *has* been a while, hasn't it?"

Bob wasn't buying it though.

"You all right?" he asked, eyeing her carefully.

"Maybe I just need to stretch out a little," she told him, standing by the ball return for her second go. If only it were that simple.

The second time was even more excruciating, though, and the results of her toss were even more disastrous as the ball again slammed into the wood floor. Even the young employee back at the cash register looked up to see what was going on.

"You need to bend down a little more, see?" Sam must have thought he was being helpful as he demonstrated the correct stance and how to release the bowling ball closer to the floor. Easy for him to say. But she smiled and nodded.

"I see what you mean. Next time."

But after just two tries Charlotte knew she couldn't finish the game. What crazy notion had made her think she could do this anyway? Even without her stiff back.

Taking care not to advertise her handicap, she made her way over to the nearby bench, where Bob joined her. They watched in silence as Christopher took his first turn. Then Bob faced her and leaned in closer.

"You're having trouble, aren't you?" he whispered.

That turned out to be the understatement of the evening. When she didn't answer right away, he leaned in even closer.

"Maybe you should go see Doc Carr. Might be more serious than you think. And all this stress you're taking on with the open house thing . . ."

"No!" She shook her head. "Doc Carr can't help."

"Now who's being stubborn? You can't always be in control of things, you know. Some things you just have to let go."

"You mean like the open house you don't want me to do?"

Charlotte bit her tongue as she felt her emotions rising once more. She could see Bob's expression cloud over as well.

"Yes!" Sam shouted as he pumped his fist in the air. "A strike! I got a strike on my first turn!"

Unfortunately neither Bob nor Charlotte had seen it, but they both clapped and cheered as a red light blinked from the ceiling above. Even the girls cheered.

But Bob wasn't finished. "Listen, Charlotte." At least he kept his voice low. "Everything can't always be perfect. The weather isn't perfect. The kids aren't perfect. Your back isn't perfect. You can't control everything, and no matter how much you try, you really can't decide what happens next, can you?"

Charlotte felt her jaw clenching. What was wrong with trying to make things as good as they could be? Was it a sin to reach for the best? Frankly, she could think of several good answers to his challenge. But with grandkids all around, she held them back.

"Grandma," Christopher looked back after taking his turn. "It's your turn again. And Grandpa, are you keeping score? I got four pins."

"Right!" Bob slipped back over to his scorecard. "Four big ones."

"Grandma . . ." Christopher repeated. But now Bob stepped up instead.

"Actually, guys, Grandma's going to sit this one out."

Charlotte thought about standing up and proving Bob wrong, but the familiar ache in her back said otherwise. Instead, she sighed in resignation.

"That's right," she told them with a wave of her hand. "I think I'd rather eat pizza and cake and let you guys do the heavy lifting. You bowl; I'll watch."

The boys looked at each other with a puzzled expression but played on. Charlotte actually felt relieved to not have to roll that awful ball down the lane anymore. What had she been thinking? One could only take so much embarrassment—and back pain, which, at this point, seemed to have a heavier hand upon her than Bob's scolding.

So instead she cheered from the sidelines, and clapped carefully when Ashley brought in their small cake with the fifteen candles. Unfortunately, even clapping made her wince. How could her silly back affect nearly everything she wanted to do?

"Watch your hair with those candles, girls," she warned them.

Emily didn't seem to hear as she blew out the candles and all her friends cheered once more.

Next would come the presents. Charlotte dug into her purse to find the card she'd written earlier that day. She didn't ask Bob if he wanted to see what they'd given Emily. She just handed it to Christopher.

"Would you please put this over by the other presents?"

He took the card and slipped it between two colorful gift bags. One, as it turned out, contained a small collection of

lip gloss and nail polish while the other had a CD pictur-
ing a handsome-looking young man that Emily seemed
especially pleased about. Next she tore open the card and
scanned the message before holding up the check.

"Wow, thanks, Grandma and Grandpa." She turned it
over before her friends could see the amount. "That's really
cool."

"You buy anything you like with it," Charlotte told her.
"Maybe a new summer outfit."

Emily nodded and slipped the check into one of her
other gift bags.

No telling how far thirty-five dollars would go, Charlotte
thought, but it was the best they could do.

Yes, Charlotte told Emily, of course it would be okay if
the girls stayed over that night. They could all sleep in
Emily's room. As long as it was okay with their parents,
that is.

Forty-five minutes later Charlotte was driving home
with four exuberant young teenage girls singing silly songs
at the top of their lungs. As it turned out, Megan had a
lovely voice and a happy smile and obviously liked to
laugh. Dark-haired Rachel didn't say as much but seemed
happy to go along with the others.

Was I really ever that young? Charlotte asked herself, keeping her back as straight and immobile as she possibly
could.

She asked herself the same question later that night as
she lay awake in bed, trying unsuccessfully to get comfortable. No matter which way she turned, her back pinched
with a vengeance and she had to move again, trying to find

a safe position. It felt as if the bed would reach up and poke her, and then she would roll from side to back to side. Punching up the pillows didn't help, and neither did Bob's steady snoring beside her. She felt her heart racing and sweat forming on her forehead.

Was he right about me, Lord? The question popped into her mind without warning as Bob's words replayed in her head: *You can't always be in control of things, Charlotte. Some things you just have to let go.*

She thought she'd done that a long time ago with Denise. But maybe now with her grandkids, she was repeating the pattern all over again. Hold on too tightly, and they pull away. Hold on too loosely, and they fall. Be in control, or not? Let them fly, or prop them up?

She could never seem to find the right balance, especially not now. Bob's snore came up short as she threw aside her covers and checked the bedside clock's glowing red numbers. She'd been awake three restless hours since they went to bed at ten. Maybe she'd eaten too much pizza, which always made her intolerably thirsty.

Enough of this. Charlotte needed something to drink. After some effort she rocked herself out of bed—all the while gritting her teeth and trying not to cry out in pain. Yes, her back felt worse—if that were possible.

Finally up, she slipped on her robe and slowly tiptoed out to the kitchen to pour herself a glass of milk. Standing in the dim light of the fridge, though, she froze at the sound of . . . giggles? At one in the morning?

Sure enough, when she stopped to listen, she heard Emily's unmistakable little laugh, joined with her friends'.

And when she looked over past the breakfast nook to the family room, a flickering green-and-blue glow told her someone was watching TV. She shuffled over for a look.

"Watch what happens next." Ashley whispered to the other three girls. They'd wrapped themselves with blankets and huddled just inches from the screen. "A hand is going to come up out of the swamp, and—"

"Shh!" The other girls came back in a chorus.

"You're going to ruin it for the rest of us," said Emily.

"Yeah!" added Megan. "I'm going to—"

Scream. They yelped and grabbed each other, and then giggled in mock horror when the hand appeared as predicted.

Charlotte quietly backed away to watch for a minute, enjoying their silliness and the way they jostled each other around. A part of her almost wished she could wrap herself up in a blanket with her girlfriends, like the girls were doing, and laugh until she cried. Because these days, and especially with this nagging, terrible pain in her back, all she could manage was the crying part.

Chapter
Twenty-Two

Y ou really don't need to spend your time like this,"
Charlotte told Hannah, who rode along in the passenger seat.

"What, you mean you don't want me to come?" Though
Hannah looked hurt, Charlotte knew her better than that.

"No, no. I'm glad you're here. It's just that you have so
much to do, getting your house back in shape. You have
enough to worry about."

Hannah sighed. "That's just it, dear. I may have enough
to worry about, but right now all the house stuff is driving
me absolutely crazy. I need to go somewhere where the
contractors can't be asking me all kinds of silly questions
about flooring and wallboard and all those things I really
don't care about. Somewhere where I don't hear hammers
pounding or saws . . . you know, doing what saws do. I
need to get away."

"I understand." Charlotte kept her eyes on the road as they
headed toward the clinic, to her appointment with Dr. Carr.

"And besides," said Hannah, "I figured since I'm the one
who talked you into seeing the doctor, I should at least
offer my moral support, right?"

"Well . . . right." Actually it was very nice of Hannah to come along.

"You know we've been praying for you, Charlotte." Hannah rested a gentle hand on Charlotte's arm. "People at church care about you."

"That's very sweet of you to say so. I do appreciate that."

Charlotte meant it. At the same time, she couldn't help thinking that perhaps they should reserve their prayers for someone who really needed them.

Charlotte was thankful that Hannah rode along without saying anything else and didn't try to fill the silence with empty chatter. She did, however, remind Charlotte that the keys were still in the ignition after they parked in front of the little whitewashed clinic and Charlotte had already struggled out of the car.

"Oh. Of course they are." Charlotte reached back inside to pluck the keys from where they dangled, but she held back a cry of pain from twisting the wrong way. "Can you tell that my mind is a thousand miles away?"

"One thing at a time. Let's get this back of yours taken care of, and then you can worry about the rest of the world."

Hannah held open the glass door as they entered the tiny waiting room filled with green, vinyl hospital chairs and little end tables piled with magazines. The only other person waiting was a young mother, obviously expecting, with a small child crawling around her feet. While Charlotte checked in, Hannah settled down behind a *People* magazine.

"She said it would be just a minute," Charlotte reported, easing herself into a chair. She smiled at the little girl, who dragged a half-dressed Barbie doll around the floor. The girl, maybe three years old, checked with her mother first, and then shyly smiled back.

"She going to have a baby too, Mama?" asked the girl. The mother smiled and shook her head.

"No, sweetheart. People come here for different reasons."

Charlotte would have laughed at the question if it didn't hurt to laugh. Instead she smiled and waited her turn after the mom and little girl were called. Ten minutes later she followed a young nurse into an examination room.

"I'm Kelley," said the nurse, who could have been Denise's age or a few years younger. Charlotte didn't remember seeing her before. "Let's get your blood pressure and a couple of preliminaries before Dr. Carr sees you. Are you all right to stand, or are you in a lot of pain?"

"Actually, if I could sit down as soon as possible, that would be nice." Charlotte hated to say it, but maybe the stress of actually coming here to the clinic was making the pain worse. "Perhaps you could help me."

"Of course, sweetheart. You just tell me if anything hurts."

Oh, she would do that, all right. But . . . *sweetheart?* Charlotte could have been this girl's mother. She tried not to shake as the chipper young nurse checked her temperature and blood pressure while prattling on about some young starlet who had won the Academy Award for best actress. Then she had Charlotte step up on the scale.

Kelley motioned to the tissue-covered exam table where Charlotte was to sit. "Dr. Carr will be with you in just a minute."

Charlotte stared at the model of the inner ear and the

lovely poster vividly chronicling the growth of unborn children. Her favorite poster was the Norman Rockwell scene of the little boy hitching up his trousers in the doctor's office. It was a cute painting, but she couldn't think of anywhere it would fit except right here in a doctor's exam room, where everything smelled of rubbing alcohol and Listerine.

Averting her eyes from the jar of cotton balls on the adjacent counter, which strangely reminded her of hypodermic needles, Charlotte had been reduced to reading the warning labels on the oxygen equipment when Dr. Carr finally came breezing in, his Mickey Mouse tie twisting around his stethoscope.

"Mrs. Stevenson, good to see you. Back pain, then?" He consulted his clipboard before beginning a series of pokes, prods, and intimate questions about recent illnesses and associated symptoms she would have preferred not to answer. No, she had not fallen recently, nor had she been in any automobile accident. No dizzy spells. She was made to walk on her heels, her toes, and the soles of her feet, movement that brought tears to her eyes.

"I'm sorry, Mrs. Stevenson." Dr. Carr sat her back on the exam bench. "You should let me know if it hurts."

"I will." She nodded and accepted his tissue. It hurt.

"You've been taking something for the pain already? Ibuprofen?"

He crossed his arms and frowned as he pulled a paper clip from his clipboard and straightened it.

"A few," she admitted.

"How about this?" he asked, poking her in the legs with

the end of the clip. "Do you feel when I do this?"

She nodded, so he went on to tap her on the knee with his hammer.

"It's better when I'm sitting down," she admitted. "But I thought perhaps you would do some X-rays." In her best medical opinion, she felt certain that would have been much easier than all this examining, would it not?

"Perhaps later, if we see a need for it. Right now I'd like to test your nerves and your muscles and then see what kind of tension we might have on your sciatic nerve."

Charlotte had no idea what a sciatic nerve might be, only that her back hurt like blazes, now more than ever, and it wasn't getting any better.

"You haven't experienced any unexplained weight loss lately?" he asked.

"That would be very nice. But unfortunately no."

"All right then." He smiled. "You still have your sense of humor. And it looks as if you haven't experienced any major signs of osteoporosis. You haven't been on steroids for any reason."

"We drink a lot of milk, but our cows are healthy."

"That's good. But you're sure about the trauma? No falls? Accidents? Trip over the dog?"

"Well, actually, it started when I tried to lift a sandbag."

Dr. Carr stopped and looked up slowly, glancing over his rather modern-looking reading glasses.

"Mrs. Stevenson, what were you doing trying to lift a sandbag?" He tapped on his clipboard now for emphasis. "All right, you don't need to answer that. But that's the kind of mild trauma I'm talking about. Or perhaps it wasn't so mild."

"Uh . . ." Charlotte wasn't sure how to explain without sounding foolish. More and more, this sounded like something Sam or Christopher would have done—certainly not her. Certainly not a sixty-something-year-old grandmother of five. She could not escape the handsome doctor's look of disapproval, no matter how much she squirmed. Actually, it hurt to squirm, and she gasped in pain as her back seized up even more.

"Hold on, there." He listened carefully now with his wickedly cold stethoscope, and then tried to hold her by the shoulder until the pain eased a bit.

"I'm sorry, Mrs. Stevenson. You're obviously in a lot of pain. For starters, let's get you something to help cut down on that."

He pulled out a pad from the breast pocket of his white lab coat and scribbled a few instructions in predictably illegible handwriting. She glanced at the pad, hoping someone else would be able to decipher the words better than she could.

"This is a prescription for a muscle relaxant. You can also soak in a hot tub or use a heating pad for some relief. If that doesn't take care of it in two or three weeks, or if the pain doesn't settle down the way I'm hoping it will, then I want you to come back and we'll see if something else is going on. All right?"

She nodded, holding her hands together so they wouldn't shake quite as much and willing herself to breathe deeply.

Settle down, girl, she told herself. There's nothing wrong with you that a hot bath and a little more rest shouldn't be able to fix.

She wanted to believe her own words, though at this point she wasn't entirely sure how much she trusted herself. What did she know about back pain? Up to now, she had thought it was just a guy problem.

"And no more lifting sandbags." Dr. Carr held out the prescription to her so there could be no mistake about the point he was trying to make. "In fact, no more lifting anything for the time being. Nothing heavier than a half-gallon of milk. Do you understand me?"

She nodded and took the paper, feeling like a scolded puppy who had just been caught next to a puddle on the kitchen floor. "I understand, but don't you think if I just put a hot pad on it—"

"As I said, you're welcome to try whatever makes you feel better." He glanced at his watch and made for the door.

"Actually . . ." She fumbled for a way to object before finally folding the prescription into the palm of her hand. No use arguing with the doctor.

"Something else?" He looked at her expectantly.

"No. Thank you, Dr. Carr."

With a smile he left her to get dressed, and she hurried as much as her back would allow. Anything to get out of there sooner rather than later. But a few minutes later she had to endure yet another lecture, this time from Edith Mosely in the back of Kepler's Pharmacy.

"Now, this is very strong, Charlotte," Edith explained, leaning over the counter and using the pill bottle to emphasize her point. "It's probably going to make you a little woozy, so no driving after you've taken it—not for at least several hours. Some people have different reactions, too, depending on how they tolerate things. I want you to read the label carefully when you get home. Be sure to take these pills with a meal, an . . ."

Charlotte couldn't keep her mind from wandering as Edith continued her instructions. No driving? That might be a problem. *If* she ended up taking the pills, that is. But she smiled and nodded earnestly before leaving the drug store with Hannah in tow. Out on the sidewalk she shivered at the chill and overcast sky, wondering when it might rain again.

"What did they give you?" asked Hannah, always the curious one.

Charlotte glanced at the bottle, turned it several ways, and tried to make out the label. Finally she handed the bottle over to her friend. "Does that look familiar to you?"

Hannah nodded as they walked. "Frank had to take it once, after his hernia operation. Really strong stuff. Scary, almost. It knocked him out and did a real number on his tummy, besides."

Well, that wasn't exactly the kind of news Charlotte wanted to hear. She could imagine trying to keep the farm going while under the influence. And what about getting ready for the open house?

This is not good timing, she told herself. *Maybe I could wait to take it.*

Her back stiffened just then, however, and the pain took her breath away. She paused in the parking lot, hoping it would settle down and allow her to move.

"Would you like me to drive, Charlotte?" Hannah meant well, but Charlotte shook her head with a little too much vigor. Even that hurt, however. Right now it hurt to breathe.

"No, no, dear," she answered between clenched teeth. "I'm not an invalid yet."

Or so she wished. Unfortunately, the stab of pain in her back as she slipped behind the steering wheel stopped her cold once again, and she blinked back tears. Having seen that, Hannah wasn't taking no for an answer. She got out of the passenger seat, walked around, and opened the driver's-side door.

"Let me help you, please." Hannah held out her hand. "You don't need to be a martyr."

"No one's ever called me that before."

"No? Well, it's about time, dear."

Charlotte thought of refusing her friend and digging in her heels, but changed her mind when her back locked up entirely. It was all she could do to look up at the unmistakably determined glint in Hannah's eye.

"All right then." She accepted her friend's hand to help her slide out and straighten up—slowly. "Just this once."

Maybe it was a good thing that Hannah had come along on this errand after all.

Chapter
Twenty-Three

Later that night Bob hunched over the disassembled parts of the water pump and squinted in the weak halo of light from the lone light bulb hanging over his cluttered workbench. An old radio set to the country station droned in the background with some cowboy singing, "How do you like me now?"

"I'll tell you how I like me now." Bob paused from his work a moment to address the radio. "Not very much."

Problem was, at this hour, his eyes refused to focus and his fingers couldn't seem to hold the tiny washer in place long enough for him to put everything all back together. The washer slipped out of his grip once again, and he bit his tongue to keep from saying something unseemly. Yes, he could use an extra hand. Where was Pete?

Probably out with the girlfriend again. And on a week-night, no less. Didn't she have to grade papers or something?

He set the rest of the parts down, rubbed his eyes, and stretched his aching neck once more. The kid was a good worker, for the most part. Pretty much always had been, even if he didn't always do things the right way, the way Bob or Bill might have done them. Thing was, Pete was always looking for shortcuts, so he didn't always see the big picture or how the little things added up.

Like this water pump here, for instance. Fix it now, and they could use the tractor again tomorrow morning, first thing. But wait until tomorrow morning to fix the problem, and they'd waste half a day's work—precious daylight, when they needed to be out in the fields.

It seemed completely obvious to Bob. Did he have to spell out what should have been common sense? No matter what Bob said to him, though—and goodness knows he'd tried every way he could think of—Pete just didn't seem to get it.

Or did he? Bob didn't turn when he heard the barn door creaking behind him, but he almost smiled.

"Just in time, Pete," he said, picking up the pieces once again. "I need another hand to help me get this pump back together. Come here. See this impeller?"

Pete didn't answer right away, so Bob had to look back to see what was up. Instead of his son, though, little Christopher stood just inside the door, shivering and holding a box in his arms.

"I don't know what an impeller is, Grandpa." He dried his nose on the sleeve of his Spiderman pajama shirt. "But maybe I can help if you tell me how."

"Oh!" Bob nearly dropped his project all over again. "I thought you were Uncle Pete."

"I know. But he's out with Dana. They went out to dinner or something in Harding. He wouldn't tell me exactly what. I don't think he's come back yet."

"That's what I thought." Bob paused for a moment. Why

not? "All right then. Put that box down and give me a hand. See this here?"

Bob showed him the washers and the gaskets, how one piece fit into another, gently, and how to turn the nuts and bolts the right way.

"Righty-tighty," he told Christopher, "and lefty-loosey."

He laughed at the sound of the words coming out of his mouth.

"I haven't thought of that in years," he admitted.

"When your dad taught you?"

Bob had to think about that.

"It's been too long ago. I don't remember."

"What else don't you remember, Grandpa?"

Again Bob had to chuckle.

"Well, if I don't remember, how could I tell you?"

Christopher eventually accepted that bit of logic as they worked on the pump. He seemed to know just how to hold things steady. Pretty good for a little guy, Bob thought. With a bit more patience and with three hands working together, they eventually reassembled the puzzle.

"Your fingers actually work pretty good," Bob told him after a few minutes. "Not as big and clumsy as mine."

"Yours aren't clumsy." Christopher held his little hand up next to his grandfather's; it fit snugly into Bob's palm. "They're just strong."

"*Hmm.* Not as strong as they used to be. Not so good at putting together old water pumps anymore. Maybe you should come out here more often."

"Maybe. But I don't know if Grandma would let me come this late."

Bob checked his watch for the first time in hours. The kid was right.

"Uh-oh. Past your bedtime, right? School night. Does she know you're out here?"

"She's asleep already. Went to bed at eight o'clock."

"At eight?" Bob knew Charlotte hadn't been feeling well since she got back from the doctor, but he had a sinking feeling she wasn't telling him the whole story.

"Yup. Turned out the lights and everything."

Well, they'd all been working hard lately. Everybody got a little stiff and sore this time of year—especially with the flooding and all. But this was something else. He couldn't even remember a time when Charlotte had been to see the doctor for something like "just a little backache." At least that's what she called it.

"Is she sick?" asked Christopher.

"No, I don't think so. Not sick exactly. Just tired, mostly."

Christopher nodded his head.

As Bob wiped his hands on a shop rag it occurred to him that his grandson had not come out to the shop to get his hands greasy or to help his grandfather. Bob nodded at the box Christopher had set on the floor.

"So what you got there?"

"My weather project for school. It's going to show how I can predict rain and stuff."

"*Hmm*. We could use some good weathermen. The folks on the TV are always getting it wrong. They don't know beans."

"I know beans. I've been reading a lot. Here, see? This is what I want to build."

Christopher reached down to the box and pulled out a

ripped page from a magazine showing a small roofed box with vents on all sides—apparently an enclosure for gauges and other weather instruments. He straightened out the wrinkles and laid it out on the workbench just under the puddle of light for Bob to see.

"Very nice." Bob nodded approvingly.

"Only I don't know how to saw, and make stuff. Sam said I'd cut off my finger if I tried, and I don't think he's telling the truth, but I really don't want to cut off my finger."

Bob had to chuckle at that one.

"No, I don't want you to either. I don't think your grandma would be too happy with us if you did."

"So does that mean you can help me?"

Bob looked at the tractor part he'd been working on, then at his watch again. The hard part was done. Tomorrow morning he and Pete could install the pump in just a few minutes, now that it was all ready to go. Of course, if Pete had helped here tonight instead of running out with the girl, they might have been closer to being done by now. But what could he do about that now?

"Let's see what you've got here."

Bob looked through Christopher's little box, then at the photo. It would be sort of like a little birdhouse, but with an opening at the top for the rain to collect in the little measuring cup. A few pieces of wood, a few screws, a little paint . . . how hard could it be? Christopher looked up at him like a little puppy dog.

"All right," Bob told him, pinning the picture up with a nail next to some of his hand tools. "Hand me that tape measure over there, would you?"

Chapter
Twenty-Four

Two days later Charlotte looked out her streaked kitchen window at the scattered clouds and trees bending in the blustery spring winds, wondering how she could ever finish cleaning things in time for the open house that weekend—particularly when she constantly felt so achy. Goodness, she could hardly even sit up in bed.

Then, for no apparent reason, she would wake up from the magazine she was reading and realize she'd been sleeping . . . again! How could a person sleep so much? It certainly wasn't because of the pills she hadn't been taking.

In fact, she struggled to remember exactly what had happened to her these past two days, laid up in bed like an invalid. The kids had helped a lot by doing their chores—at least she thought they had. They'd fed the dog, who moped underfoot as if understanding that something was wrong. Pete had volunteered to do most of the cooking, and she'd actually let him. After all, what was the worst he could do to frozen food?

But she wasn't hungry, lying in bed when she should have been up and busy. Nothing tasted good.

And what about Bob? When he wasn't working on spring planting or helping their neighbors prepare their equipment, he seemed to be missing in action. In fact, the past several evenings he'd disappeared for hours at a time. To where? She wanted to ask him if he'd picked up a new hobby or something. But he was up and out before she awoke each morning, and more often than not he was still gone when she fell asleep again each night.

Same as Pete, who now acted busier than she'd ever seen him. Where he used to hang around the kitchen and chat, and where he had once seemed to have all the time in the world, now he gulped down a glass of milk and ran back out into the gloomy overcast.

At least that's what she remembered, sort of, since everything seemed as gloomy and foggy as her daily, well, *stupor*. She was so tired she had to lie down again.

Maybe I should just take those stupid pills, after all. She closed her eyes for a moment and wondered where she had left the unopened bottle. Even if she did decide to take them, she couldn't imagine getting much groggier. If she finally took them, at least then maybe the pain would go away.

"No!" She scolded herself out loud and shifted once again to find a more comfortable position. Was that a raised lump in the middle of her mattress, or just a rumpled sheet? She wasn't sure, but she did know she was sick and tired of being sick and tired.

She had never wasted even nine hours sleeping every night, not to mention the naps—an hour or two at a time, and far too often. They only seemed to make her drowsier than ever, leaving her groggy and listless as she read magazines, or the Scriptures, or tried to knit. At the moment, nothing seemed appealing.

Once in a while, when no one else was home, she would venture out of bed to start a small job here and there, like dusting or straightening up the kitchen. But it usually hurt too much to stand, and she never got anything useful done before realizing she had to go lie down again.

How would they ever be ready to host an open house? The yard remained a soggy mess, strewn with broken branches and debris from the rains. Faded green paint on the shed still peeled. And still Bob was nowhere to be seen.

Does anyone know what I'm going through? She shook her head to clear her brain, but that turned out to be a poor idea.

The whole rotten open house affair reminded her too much of her pie-baking fiasco last Thanksgiving, when she'd admittedly taken on far too much. When would she ever learn not to promise what she couldn't deliver? Then, as now, too many people were depending on her—people who were going to be disappointed. And then, as now, she didn't want to be there when it all came tumbling down on her head.

The way it was doing right now. She wondered if the pain would ever leave her. As she bent over the sink she caught a distorted glimpse of her face in the shiny doughnut of the sink's drain.

"Dear me!" she gasped, wondering if the frightful apparition in the sink was really her.

Chapter
Twenty-Five

Nearly a half hour later, Charlotte caught herself still staring into the kitchen sink.

She wondered how she must appear these days to Bob and the kids, as she was always wearing the same bathrobe, now with jam stains on the front, and her hair was a jumbled mess.

Speaking of which, what had happened to Sam and Emily? She looked out the window again and spied a movement around the side of the barn, where someone out there was . . . raking the lawn?

Another look told her Christopher had earnestly attacked the mess left behind by the floods, with mixed results. Behind Christopher, Emily came trundling a wheelbarrow; she scooped up an armload of sticks and soggy leaves.

That left only Sam, who a short time later appeared from around the corner of the shed, ladder in hand. He bumped the end into Christopher's leg—accidentally or on purpose. Even from inside the house, though, she heard Christopher squawk.

Well, this was very sweet of them. But even Charlotte knew they had all bitten off way more than they could chew. With so many things yet to do, even the four of them would not be able to spruce up the farm in time.

She felt duty-bound to go out there and encourage them—rather than escape back to her bed. *I have to go out there*, she told herself, taking a deep breath. *Never mind this old woman's back.*

If she did, perhaps she could apologize for . . . for being the way she was. So she left the pills back in her bedroom, pulled a sweater off the hook by the back door, and stepped out gingerly with Toby into a brisk April wind, which sent a shiver up her spine and swirled last fall's leaves from under the steps. She took a deep breath, careful not to strain her back all over again, and enjoyed the scents of green and wet. The rain had stopped—for now—but low clouds overhead threatened to dump even more.

"You're up!" Pete emerged from the barn with Stormy in tow, and his face lit up. "We all thought you were sleeping in again today."

She tried to sound as normal as she could, even worked up a pleasant expression.

"You must think I sleep for a living."

"You doing better now, Grandma?" asked Christopher as he trundled by with an armload of leaves. She wished she owned just a fraction of the optimism in his voice. "'Cause yesterday you looked pretty bad."

"I'll take that as a compliment, considering how I must still appear this morning." Once again Charlotte tried her best to smile as she reached out to give her grandson a quick squeeze. "Actually, Mom," Pete chimed in, "Dad's been really worried about you. Talks about you all the time. So we're getting your to-do list done."

Well, that would have been nice, if it were true. But her skeptical look must have come across more obviously than she would have liked.

"You're acting like it's a huge shock." He gripped Stormy's halter and looked her straight in the eye. "Maybe you never thought of asking for help?"

Stormy whinnied, and she wasn't sure how to answer, or even quite what he meant, until he pointed in the direction of the driveway. As if on cue, a large flatbed truck loaded with hay bales pulled into the drive and was bouncing in their direction, honking its horn. Three young teens waved as they approached. A pickup followed closely behind, then a large Suburban and a smaller truck. Each vehicle in the parade looked full to overflowing with teens.

Oh no! But since Charlotte knew she wouldn't be able to move back inside quickly enough, she decided to greet the guests as if she always looked this way.

Sam looked particularly interested in the guests, especially as a pretty girl with raven-black hair pulled back into a ponytail stepped off the last truck. If Charlotte were a gambler—which she was not, but if she were—she'd put money on the fact that Sam had a crush. She could tell by the off-center grin that crossed his face.

"Something tells me you know what these young people are doing here," said Charlotte, backing slowly toward the door.

But Pete didn't explain, and Charlotte couldn't make her feet move quickly enough. A few moments later a young man about Pete's age unfolded his tall frame from the last truck and approached. Charlotte recognized him as a teacher from the high school but couldn't recall his name.

His crew began unloading equipment, tools, and cans of paint from the trucks.

"We're in the right place, aren't we?" asked the man, shaking Pete's hand.

"Hey, Tim," answered Pete, smiling broadly. "You're a lifesaver."

"Well, it really wasn't that hard when I told my kids they'd be getting extra credit for coming out after school today."

He held out his hand to Charlotte.

"Mrs. Stevenson, I'm Tim Copeland, the FFA adviser. I don't know if we've ever officially met."

So that was it. The Future Farmers of America to the rescue.

"I'm sorry, I . . ." She hesitated to smooth back her hair, knowing it wouldn't make any difference at this point. "I've been resting."

"Oh, that's okay, Mrs. Stevenson."

He smiled, and she shook his hand as Pete explained how he'd called around for help the other day. He and Tim hadn't been in the same class, together, but . . .

"But you know, Mrs. Stevenson, this is the kind of thing we like to do. A couple of my kids had their homes damaged in the flooding, so we all know what it's like. We all need a little extra help once in a while, right?"

But that was only the beginning. Within minutes three more truckloads of FFA kids arrived, bringing paint sprayers and brushes, buckets and rakes, hammers and toolboxes. Charlotte went inside to change and brush her hair, and then couldn't help coming back out to the porch to see exactly what was going on. Actually, the fresh air seemed to help her lingering headache more than anything else, and even her back pain seemed to back off just a little.

Well, she told herself, *it does me good to see the kids' friends pitch in.* Like Sam's friends Jake and Paul, and Ashley. By then even Dana Simons had arrived to help Pete hand out work assignments, and she immediately seemed to know which kids could handle which jobs.

"I hope you don't mind us sort of taking over like this, Mrs. Stevenson." Dana looked up from her clipboard with an apology on her sweet, round face, and then pointed out a fence that needed scraping and painting to a couple of the kids. Now she sounded more like the English teacher than Pete's . . . special friend. "It just seemed like the easiest way to get things done."

"Not at all!" Charlotte looked around the yard at the energetic teens hurrying to their assignments, tools in hand. "But how did you know?"

Dana brushed her straight, dark hair back from her eyes and looked at Pete to explain, though actually there was no need. Dana easily matched Pete in height, and her shoulder brushed easily up against his. They reminded Charlotte of an old married couple, each seeming to know what the other would say before he or she said it.

"Mom," Pete explained, "it's not that hard to make a to-do list, all right? I learned from the list master."

Dana laughed as yet another car pulled into the driveway, and her broad smile seemed genuine.

"Speaking of list masters . . ." Pete pointed to the unexpected visitor. By that time there was hardly any space left for Bill to park close to the house. Charlotte's older son carefully squeezed his Toyota sedan between two trucks and climbed out to join them. Anna and the girls piled out of the car, as well.

"I got your voice mail, little brother," said Bill. "Hey, Mom. You feeling better?"

He slipped on a brand-new red-and-white Nebraska Huskers ball cap with a capital N in front, rolled up the sleeves of his nicely pressed light blue dress shirt, and stepped carefully around a puddle in the gravel, avoiding Toby's inquisitive sniffing. Sometimes Charlotte wondered if he and Pete were actually brothers. But when they stood next to each other, no one could miss the resemblance. They both looked like their father, but each in his own way.

"So where's Dad?" wondered Bill, checking his Rolex and looking around the farm.

Pete nodded silently toward the Sawchuck's Quarter, where a distant chugging sound and small flock of birds told them their father would still be preparing the fields for planting, even if no one else was.

"Hey," chirped Christopher, pointing toward the tractor, "that might be our seagull again."

"That's our good luck," said Bill. "We don't get that very often. Must have been blown in by the storm. Lost."

But Christopher shook his head in disagreement. "Grandma says there's no such thing as luck, Uncle Bill."

"Oh really? My mistake."

"And he's not lost. The seagull, I mean. He's just where he's supposed to be. Right, Uncle Pete?"

Pete shifted nervously and pulled the bill of his frayed, weathered cap lower on his forehead.

"Actually," he mumbled, "I need to get back out there and help him pretty quick."

"Hey, not a problem." Bill clapped his hands. "We'll cover for you. I brought the glass for the back door that needs fixing, the way you said. Let's get this party started!"

Charlotte wasn't sure she would have called it a party, except that all the FFA kids treated it that way. And it was probably a good thing Bob wasn't there yet to see how much white paint they spilled on themselves, compared with how much actually made it onto the shed and the barn. But with so many hands helping, and a paint sprayer that made a considerable amount of noise as it filled the air with a white paint cloud, well, she couldn't complain.

Sam didn't seem to be complaining about any of the work either. In fact, he and the girl with the raven-colored hair seemed to be having quite a good time painting a corner of the shed together.

"Uh, Pete?" Charlotte pulled him off to the side and lowered her voice. "Who's that girl over there with Sam?"

"You know." Pete hardly looked before answering. "The Friesen girl. Arielle. Her dad's a sheriff's deputy."

"So are they—"

"I know NOTHING!" Pete made a show of shaking his head and zipping his lip, but it was plain to Charlotte that he must have known the whole story. Well, she would have to find out a little later.

Pete turned his attention back to the sprayers.

"Whoa!" He parked his hands on his hips and watched their progress. "I've never seen a shed painted this quick before."

A new load of gravel was being spread quickly across the

parking area. Never mind the way two of the boys had to repark all the cars and trucks to get them out of the way. Charlotte closed her eyes as gravel and paint flew in all directions. Better not to know all the details sometimes.

The picket fence got painted, and the windows washed —twice. Once before the pressure washers on the roof sent moss flying in all directions, and again after. Hinges on the larger barn door were replaced (only a little bit crooked), trim on the side of the house was fixed, and broken branches from several of the driveway elms were trimmed and hauled away to the burn pile.

And that was just a start. Bill made quick work of repairing the shattered glass in the back door, every flower and plant that had been destroyed by the rains was replaced, and a dozen new flower boxes were hung around both the front and back porches. Anna even helped rake gravel, looking like an ad for *House Beautiful* with her sunglasses and brightly colored aqua scarf. The kids strategically placed hay bales in front of a muddy area, creating a nice country border for the lawn.

"A little farther to the left?" Charlotte called out, and the boys looked to her as she waved directions from her safe spot by the back door.

With every job completed—even with paint that ran or beams that appeared a little less than level—Charlotte finally saw her elephant shrinking. Before she knew what time it was, Hannah showed up with an armload of boxed pizzas.

"Cool!" Emily crowded in around the picnic table by the back door with the rest of them. "We haven't had pizza in ages!"

Charlotte supposed that to a teenager, even two days could probably seem like "ages." She slipped into the kitchen to find herself a yogurt in the refrigerator. And she gazed out at the Sawchuck's Quarter, wondering if Bob would ever take a break.

Chapter
Twenty-Six

By that Thursday afternoon, Charlotte was more than ready to take a break from baking chocolate chip cookies. Maybe another nap would be good, though she didn't want to remind herself how much time she'd spent flat on her back in bed for the past week. What could she do about it? She wiped the flour from her hands as Christopher burst in from outside, followed by a rush of chilly air.

"What's cooking, Grandma?" He tossed his backpack on the kitchen table and reached for one of the cookies cooling on a paper towel. "I can smell 'em from all the way outside."

She grabbed for his hand to stop him, but too late.

"These are for the school groups coming here this weekend," she told him. "Not for us."

"I'm in a school group," he answered, stuffing a gooey treat into his mouth and licking the chocolate off his fingers. Charlotte successfully fended him off from snatching any more cookies.

"You may be in a school group, but that's the last cookie you're having, mister. Don't want to spoil your appetite, do you?"

"Sure I do." He smiled at her with a chocolate-smudged grin, and she could only sigh.

"Why did I ask? I tell you what. Why don't you go out and find your grandpa. Tell him we're going to have dinner a little early, today."

"He in Sawchuck's?"

"I don't know. Haven't seen him—or your Uncle Pete, for that matter—all afternoon. But go on. I'm sure you'll find them."

"And then can I have another cookie?"

She scooted him out the door with a gentle swat.

"After dinner; I have a couple of broken ones. Now go."

CHRISTOPHER CHECKED FIRST by the horses, then by the chicken coop. No Grandpa and no Uncle Pete.

I need one of those remote-control drone flying things with a camera, he thought. *Then I could find them no matter where they are. Take spy pictures of the whole farm.*

But right now he had to find Grandpa and Uncle Pete without a remote-control flying camera drone. As soon as he turned from the chicken coop he heard a faint chugging sound that gave him a good clue.

Here they come! He turned his head north to see Grandpa's old tractor approaching the farm along Heather Creek Road, with Uncle Pete riding shotgun on the side. No wonder Grandma hadn't seen them anywhere. They'd probably been off at a neighbor's farm, helping with the planting the way they'd been doing lately. He waved as they came closer and eventually pulled up next to the barn.

"Hey, Christopher-man." Uncle Pete hopped to the ground as the tractor sputtered to a stop. "What's up?"

"Grandma sent me out to find you," replied Christopher. "Something about early dinner."

"Perfect." Uncle Pete made for the barn. "I'm starving."

"You're always starving," added Grandpa, climbing off his tractor a bit more slowly, as if his legs didn't bend the same way his son's did. But he motioned for Christopher to follow him into the barn.

"Is the paint dry?" wondered Christopher, squinting in the dim light filtering through the cracks. Uncle Pete was already standing by the workbench inside and had flipped on the buzzing overhead light.

"I've been wondering, myself," answered Grandpa. Uncle Pete poked at the little blue-painted structure that reminded Christopher of an oversized birdhouse, only this was much better.

"Pretty cool, I'd say." Uncle Pete admired their handi-work. Or mostly Grandpa's, actually. "You paint this your-self, Christopher?"

Christopher shook his head and pointed to the white trim.

"I painted that part."

The three of them stood there for a minute to admire their handiwork. Grandpa had built the little house with a tiny front porch and tiny windows with real panes, a tiny front door and a tiny shingled roof that opened up on a hinge—with a hole in the middle of the roof for the rain to drop through, right into the glass with the markings to show how much had fallen. The unit would sit on a sturdy four-by-four post about four feet tall.

"So you gonna set this up for the open house?" asked Uncle Pete. By this time Grandpa had found something else to putter with on his workbench. All Christopher could do was shrug and nod.

"It's going to be a hit," said Uncle Pete, patting Christopher on the shoulder. "As long as the weather clears up."

"It'll be nice." He crossed his arms to show that he was sure, because he was. "It's going to be great weather. I guarantee it."

"Well, glad you're sure." Uncle Pete obviously wasn't buying it that easily. "But you know, sometimes the weather doesn't do what we think it's . . ."

Uncle Pete didn't finish what he was saying, as they heard Emily shouting from outside the barn.

"Grandpa!" she yelled, yanking open the barn door. "Grandpa, are you in there? I think you'd better come. Grandma did something to her back again!"

This time Grandpa's legs moved more quickly than Christopher had seen them move before as he hurried out of the barn and back to the house. Christopher and Uncle Pete followed right on his heels.

"I FEEL SILLY," Charlotte told them from where she sat at the kitchen table. "I was just gathering a couple of little potatoes, like I've done a thousand times before, and . . ."

She really didn't want to go into all the details about the full sack she'd foolishly tried to lift from the pantry. Nor did she want to tell them how her back had once more felt like a piano string stretched to the snapping point without fair warning.

Unfortunately, the potatoes strewn all over the kitchen's linoleum floor gave everyone a pretty good idea of what had happened.

You'd think I would have known better, she told herself.

"Boys, let's pick these up." Bob now took charge, directing Pete, Sam, and Christopher to help. Emily went to the sink for a damp washcloth

"Really," said Charlotte. "I just need a moment to catch my breath. No need to make such a fuss."

"All right then." Bob leaned in to mop her forehead with Emily's washcloth as if she had a fever and not a strained back. Charlotte gasped at another spasm of pain and felt her eyes widening in panic.

"Grandma?" Christopher looked at her with concern, a potato in each hand. "You don't look so good."

"Don't you . . . worry about me." She managed to pat him on the arm. "I'm fine."

But at this point her words sounded quite preposterous, given the obvious. And the kids would know better than to believe her, though she felt obliged not to fall flat on her back in the middle of the kitchen. Such a sight, she imagined, would not be a pleasant one.

"You're not even close to fine," Bob told her. "Now let's see if I can get you up."

"Please don't . . . ," she told them with a raised hand as Bob and Christopher helped her to the door. She meant to add "worry about me," but once again her voice failed her.

Her husband misunderstood. "No arguing," he told her. "I'll get you a hot pad. But really, you need to go to bed."

Well, naturally she was going to bed. But the real problem,

now that she thought about it, was much larger than making a scene here in the kitchen.

What about this weekend? she asked herself.

Yes, and what about all the school groups and the buses full of kids coming all the way from Harding and who knows where?

What about the cleanup she still needed to do, or the cookies she had to set out, or even all the tours of the farm they would have to lead?

"I know what you're thinking," Bob finally told her as he walked her slowly to their room. He swung the door closed behind them, and it clicked shut. "So you just give me the name of that Farm Family lady, and I'll call her tonight, tell her to call off everything."

"No, Bob. Please. We can't do that."

"What do you mean, we can't?" Bob frowned as he helped her sit on the edge of the bed. "You can't be up and running around. You can't direct people, the way you always do. You can't do *anything*."

His words stung, even if they were true. He was right.

"I don't know about the up-and-running-around part," she answered. "All I know is, it's way too late to cancel. We'll figure out some way to pull it off. Can't you see how important it is?"

"Not really. We'll do fine without the gift certificates."

"Robert James Stevenson! You know it's not about the gift certificates."

"No? Then what's it about?"

"It's about the kids." She lowered her voice now so the rest of the family, still out in the kitchen, wouldn't hear.

"That's all it's ever been about. Giving them a reason to be proud of their home—and no, *pride* is not a bad word. Not this kind of pride."

"Didn't know there was more than one kind."

"Well, I may not be a Bible scholar, but I just don't think it's the same as 'pride' in the Bible. You, of all people, should know that."

Bob should also know when Charlotte was determined to do something, or to finish what she had begun. She sat stubbornly on the edge of her bed, waiting for him to either agree or not while he paced the floor of their bedroom. He would wear a hole in the little yellow area rug, she thought. Finally he stopped and rubbed the stubble on his chin.

"All right," he said, his voice also lower. "So if we *do* open up the farm to the whole world, we still don't know how many will show up, do we?"

Charlotte thought it far too late to be talking about this event hypothetically, but for now she went along with him.

"We take one day at a time," she answered, and couldn't help the sinking feeling that she was collapsing into clichés. "All the kids will have to lend a hand, and we'll get this over with."

Get through it. Get it over with. She wiped away a tear, wondering why she was the only one who seemed to take this seriously.

"I'm sorry, Bob," she finally told him. "Maybe we should never have agreed to all this."

"We?" This time he didn't look at her as he headed for the door, but she knew just what he was getting at.

Another time, she might have snapped back at his words. But right now she was spent. Her head ached, her back throbbed, and all she wanted to do was crawl under the covers. To sleep. To hide.

Again.

CHARLOTTE SLEPT and hid in her bed much longer than she intended, emerging only late the next morning to see about fixing breakfast for the kids. The alarm must not have sounded, for some reason.

Again she must have looked a sight, and she was even afraid to look in the mirror as she practically crawled past Toby's welcome and out to the kitchen. Pete, however, intercepted her.

"Mom! Where do you think you're going after your meltdown last night?" He held out his hands to steady her, literally keeping her from falling.

"I wouldn't call it that," she told him. "Now if you'll excuse me, I have to fix breakfast for the kids and get them off to school."

"That's all taken care of." He turned her back in the direction of her room. "You just go back to bed, where you belong."

"But what about tomorrow?" She tried to protest. "The open house. All the kids coming. We're not nearly ready yet. Nothing is ready yet. It's not going to happen if I don't get up."

"Yes, it is. We're going to handle it."

"But—"

"Mom, would you stop worrying? I told you we'll handle it, so we'll handle it. You're not in any shape to be doing any of this."

"Maybe so," she managed, "but . . ."

"But nothing. Now go back to bed. Or do I have to carry you?"

"You don't have to be rude about it." This time she allowed him to help her to the door. But she was not at all confident that Pete could deliver on his promise, even if he had coordinated the planting of most of the area farms.

At the moment, however, she had little choice. She didn't want to seem like a hypochondriac, and she certainly would not tell anyone else in the family, but now her stomach had decided to shrivel and churn as well. So all she could do just then was crawl back into bed and curl up into a ball. She didn't even look up when she heard a soft knock on the bedroom door a few minutes later.

"Mom?" asked Pete, poking his nose inside. "Sorry to bother you, but there's one more thing."

"Huh?" Charlotte couldn't even open her eyes.

"I need you to tell me a little more about the farm."

"The farm?" He made no sense—none whatever. "What are you talking about?"

"I just mean, like, if I was going to write a history of the farm."

"You know as much as I do."

"No, I don't. I mean, I know Dad told me some stories when I was little. But I never really paid all that much attention. And now if I mention it at all, he never really wants to get into the details."

"So what do you need to know?"

"Okay, like, did Grandma Mildred ever tell you when the barn was built, that sort of thing?"

Charlotte thought she had, but right now her brain wasn't exactly working at its peak. Pete asked her question after question, but in her current state Charlotte could neither recall the answers nor understand why he was asking them. After two or three more questions, she had to know.

"It's just for, you know, tours and stuff. Julie Gauge wanted to know, and when I meet with her—"

"Wait a minute. You're meeting with the Farm Family lady?"

"Well. Yeah. She's coming by in a couple hours to make sure everything's okay."

Charlotte started to sit up at the news, but Pete wouldn't let her.

"Don't worry, Mom. I already told her you weren't feeling too good. I'm going to meet with her. We're going to take care of everything."

But . . . would he?

THAT AFTERNOON CHRISTOPHER clutched his box and looked up at the dark clouds as he waited for his brother to pick him up out in front of the school.

Hope I was right about it not raining tomorrow, he told himself. To tell the truth, he wasn't feeling quite as confident about clear skies for Saturday, the way he'd predicted. Maybe Uncle Pete had been right. Sometimes the weather just didn't do what we hoped, no matter what. He jumped as Sam pulled up in his rusty little car and honked the horn.

"Throw your junk in back," Sam told him when Christopher opened the passenger door. "We've gotta hurry."

Christopher slipped into the front seat and found a place in the back for his box.

"Why? We have to pick up your girlfriend?"

"No, we don't, squirt." Sam playfully punched his little brother in the arm. "And she's not my girlfriend . . . exactly."

"Ow!" Christopher yelped. But he knew he'd scored a point when Sam's cheeks reddened a bit. "So where's Emily? And what's your rush?"

"Emily got a ride with another friend. And the rush is that since Grandma hurt her back again, Uncle Pete's being a slave driver. He says we have to finish cleaning up the whole farm by ourselves."

"Think we can?" Christopher buckled his seat belt as they zipped away from the school a little too fast. Sam shook his head.

"Don't tell him I said so. But there's not a chance. Not the way Grandma wants."

Chapter
Twenty-Seven

Charlotte had no idea how she'd slept through the alarm again the next day. Saturday, of all days! But by the time she rolled over to see the other side of the bed empty, the sun was blazing in through the freshly scrubbed window, and the clock showed 7:30.

"Bob?" She frantically felt his pillow to make sure he wasn't really there. He would not be—not this late. In fact, Bob's side was cold, and his sheets were pulled neatly up— the way he might have done if she weren't still asleep. For a minute she lay still and blinked at the brightness, having nearly forgotten what it was like to wake up with sunshine. She listened for signs of life.

Nothing yet. At least her head had stopped hammering, and for the first time in days her back felt—well, it almost seemed to feel normal again.

"Thank you, Lord," she whispered. With a smile at the sunshine, she eased out of bed, slipped on her robe, and shuffled out of her room to see what had happened in the outside world. She even stretched her back just a bit, testing to see how far she could move. *Hmm.* Quite stiff, yes, but so far, it felt downright good again to be alive.

As long as she didn't try to lift any more sacks of potatoes.

"Is anyone awake out here?" she asked, still blinking in the sunshine.

No one answered, though her first surprise was that someone had actually done the breakfast dishes. The table had been cleared, and several bowls and juice glasses neatly lined the drying rack next to the sink. Amazing. Who had done such a thing without Charlotte there to remind them?

She looked around the kitchen, just to be sure she wasn't dreaming. The pile of newspapers by the back door? Gone. Three pairs of shoes had been straightened and lined up on a floor mat. Several oversized winter coats that had been hanging on the coat tree were gone, apparently put away for the season. The floor had obviously been scrubbed of muddy footprints and dog slobber, and now it smelled vaguely of Lysol. And a vase of beautiful golden daffodils graced the counter by the stove.

"I've died and gone to heaven," she whispered. But she jumped when the back door burst open. She then turned to stand face-to-face with Christopher.

"Grandma!" Eyes wide, he looked just as surprised to see her as she probably did him. "I didn't mean to wake you up. I'm sorry. Grandpa said no noise. I'm . . ."

"You're fine, little man." She almost had to laugh at his startled expression. "But Grandpa said not to wake me up? That was . . ."

Unexpected.

Christopher nodded. "He said we're all supposed to help and that we should let you sleep as long as you wanted. So I was supposed to tiptoe when I came inside to the bathroom."

"Well, as you can see, I'm already awake. So you just make all the noise you want. And, just curious, who did all the breakfast dishes without me asking?"

"Yours truly." Christopher smiled and bowed, suddenly behaving quite theatrically. He straightened and nodded toward the back door. "We've been pretty busy, even though Sam said we wouldn't be able to finish everything in time. And did you notice something else, Grandma?"

Charlotte noticed but didn't let on.

"You took off your muddy shoes before you came in the house?"

Of course he had not, but he pointed toward the door again for emphasis.

"Come on, Grandma. You can see!"

Charlotte pretended not to understand for yet another moment, and then opened her mouth in mock surprise.

"Oh! You mean the sunshine here on the day of the open house? I did notice. Good job."

"Don't thank me. I didn't do it. I just predicted it."

"Absolutely you did. In fact, I don't know how all the meteorologists on TV got it wrong, but you sure got it right, didn't you?"

Christopher smiled again and disappeared around the corner before she could ask him what else was going on outside. She would grab a banana and see for herself, poking her head out the back door into the glorious sunshine.

Actually, "glorious" hardly did it justice. She closed her eyes and took a deep breath, relishing the scent of new life, green and growing. Of flowers planted and seeds awakening. Most of all, things seemed to smell of brilliant light beyond the clouds. Charlotte knew if she stood there long enough with the sun shining on her face, it would do for her what all the pills and doctors could not.

"Hey, Mom!" Pete interrupted her deep breathing as he yelled down at her from the open second-story window of his apartment over the tractor shed. "You're up!"

"I most certainly am," she answered, opening her eyes and pulling her robe a little tighter around her. Despite the sun, she felt a touch of chill in the air. "You didn't think I would be sleeping all day, did you?"

He looked down at her with his head cocked to the side. "You really want me to answer that?"

"All right, fine; I guess I don't. What's happening out here?"

A phone rang from Pete's apartment, and he held up his hand.

When he'd finished the call, he turned back to her with a smile.

"Pete, what have you been doing?" she asked.

"Nothing much." He shrugged. "I just told the Scouts to be here by nine," he said, checking his watch. "They're going to direct traffic. And then the youth groups and the ladies from church come at nine thirty; they're cooking all the hamburgers. Julie got the county Extension Service's master gardeners to set up a table too, but they don't have to be here that early."

"Julie?"

"Gauge. Julie Gauge. You remember."

"Yes, of course. But why don't you come down here and tell me, instead of shouting out your window?"

"Sure, Mom. But I've just got to tell you: everything starts at eleven. The open house is from eleven to five."

"And Dana?" She couldn't help but ask.

"Oh, yeah. She's going to be helping me and Dad with the tours when all the school kids roll in. She'll be here in a few."

"In a few" turned out to be not more than twenty minutes later, as Dana Simons came rolling up the driveway in a black pickup and Pete trotted out to meet her. They probably didn't know Charlotte saw them kiss as she peeked through the kitchen window. But by that time, she was dressed, and she hurried outside once again to see what she could do.

"Grills over there in the middle of the lawn!" Pete directed traffic as his helpers started to arrive. "We want the booth set up there in front of it, so people can just walk on by."

Several men unloaded three large propane grills and followed his directions. Another pickup pulled up with a pile of folding tables, all marked with "BCC," no doubt borrowed from the basement of the Bedford Community Church. Still another truck arrived with a large, wooden platform and a sound system complete with large speakers on man-sized stands. Charlotte shook her head in amazement.

"Where did you find time to organize all this?" she asked her son. He whisked by with a large speaker in his arms.

"I told you," he answered. "Julie Gauge helped me make a few phone calls. Didn't have too much problem convincing people to help, especially when they knew what happened with your back."

"Oh, Pete. There are families around here with far worse problems than an aching back, don't you think? What about all the spring planting your father has been working so hard on? And the rebuilding of those flooded homes?"

"I dunno, Mom. That all may be so. But whether you know it or not, people around here really love you. You and Dad both. Did you know that Dad called the prayer chain for you after your meltdown the other night?"

"He did?" What was she supposed to say to that? Just then Bill emerged from the barn with a folding chair, and he set it up for her near the barn door.

"You ought to rest a minute, Mom." He dusted it off for her. "Sit here with the dog. Take it easy on that back. No lifting."

"Bill? Where did you come from?"

"What do you mean?" he gave her a puzzled look. "Anna and the kids and I have been here since . . ." He checked his watch. "Well, we've been here a few minutes."

She smiled at the fact that he and his family were actually here. And he pointed once more at the chair.

"Dad said we need to keep an eye on you, that you'd probably be up and trying to overdo it. So it's my official job as mayor of River Bend to make sure you take it easy. Understand? Don't want that old back to start acting up, again."

"I'll have you know that 'old back' is . . ." She was about to say "fine" but changed her mind. Truth be told, her knees felt a little wobbly, even if she did feel 90 percent better than the day before. Better make that 80 percent. She settled for thanking him and then sat down to watch.

"Speaking of your father," she said, "where is he? And what else is he telling you to do?"

Almost before the words left her mouth, Bob emerged from around the back of the barn, driving a tractor pulling a cart loaded with a rather large . . . well, it looked like a booth of some kind. Painted a jaunty bright yellow with white trim, it reminded her of something one might find at the Adams County Fair. It was large enough to tip precariously from side to side whenever Bob hit a bump.

"Gangway!" He waved as he pulled the booth out into the sunshine, and his two sons directed him to a place in the middle of the lawn, in front of the grills and beneath the shade of several elm trees. One of the cart's wheels sank in a patch of soft ground and nearly sent the booth tumbling. But they caught it in time, and with the help of several other men lowered it into place. Charlotte couldn't resist easing herself out of the chair and coming over to see as Bob silenced the tractor's motor and stood beside her, admiring the booth himself.

"Where did this come from?" she asked. She ran her hand along one of the uprights to where a cute little overhang made it look like the booth had a shingled roof. Someone had taken great care in its building, and she had a sneaking suspicion who.

"Built it during all the spare time I've been having lately. Can't be bored around here, you know." Bob straightened the booth's front counter and pretended to look dead serious. He could not fool her in that regard, however. She could see the surreptitious grin playing at the corners of his mouth.

"You?" She parked her hands on her hips and once more put on her most surprised look. Only this time, she could claim genuine surprise. "Whatever happened to 'Pride goeth before a fall'?"

Charlotte bit her tongue. She hadn't meant to challenge him again that way; it just slipped out.

Without warning, Bob took her by the hand and gently pulled her away from the booth and the people and into the shadows of the barn.

What is this all about?

He squared her shoulders in his hands and helped her sit on a bale of hay. Sunlight streamed in through cracks in the board siding, catching him in the face. This time she couldn't quite tell the emotion behind the serious look, but he crossed his arms and took a deep breath before launching into what he had to say.

"Listen to me, Charlotte," he began. "You know I didn't want to do this whole open house thing, right from the start. I still don't think it's a great idea, on the whole."

"Then . . . ?" She waited for him to explain further.

"Then I saw how the kids are, you know, pitching in. The way we always wanted 'em to. Even Jennifer and Madison are running around here, helping out."

"Seems to me that's more Pete's doing, and maybe your own. I don't have too much to do with that," she said.

"You're the one who pushed for this." He waved toward the yard, where everyone milled about, setting up booths and such. "And Pete, you know he's kind of taken this on these past days. He's been on the phone, calling everybody he can think of, asking them to come help."

"I actually *hadn't* noticed, until this morning," she admitted a little sheepishly.

"Well, that's fine. You haven't been out of bed for a while."

"You're right about that. But you still don't think it's a good idea. Then why—"

"Look," he interrupted, "What I'm trying to say is that you were right, and I was wrong. What else do you want? Do I have to get down on one knee, the way I did when I proposed?"

By this time Charlotte thought she could risk a tiny smile. After all, they both remembered his proposal to her all those years ago, kneeling in the grass down by Heather Creek. How could she forget? And how could she not smile?

"What?" he asked, looking hurt. "Is something funny?"

"You are." She reached up to stroke his grizzled cheeks, making him smile for the first time in . . . in a long time. "You're funny. You may not know it, but you're funny."

"Hmph. Wasn't trying to be. Just trying to make things clear."

"Oh, you're very clear, Mr. Stevenson. Let me see if I got this straight. I'm right, and you're wrong. The open house is going to be good for the kids."

He tried to look serious again but didn't pull away. Instead, he leaned in close, the way that usually made Charlotte's heart beat a little faster. Never mind that they'd been married forty-five years.

"You know I hate arguing with you," he told her, only inches away. She nodded. "Fact, there's nothing I hate more."

"You're not very good at it either," she told him.

"So why are we doing something all the time that neither of us wants to do? Why have we been arguing so much?"

So Christopher had been right about them, and she'd known it all along. His words echoed in her remembering: *You act like you're mad at each other all the time . . .*

Charlotte started to open her mouth, thinking for a moment that she might defend herself. But as it turned out, she really didn't have a good answer. In this case, she realized, there could be no good answer. Excuses, perhaps. But no good answer.

"I have no idea why we've been arguing so much," she finally managed, her voice breaking. "So is this a truce?"

"Nope." He shook his head, looking as if he was about to tell one of his jokes. "Truce is temporary. I'm going for a full-blown peace treaty."

Even after forty-five years, Charlotte had to admit Bob Stevenson knew how to get her attention.

"I'm sorry, Bob," she whispered, wrapping her arms around him and returning his affection.

"I'm sorrier. But if you quote me in public, I'll deny every word."

"So then what *were* we arguing about?"

"I don't remember." This time when he grinned at her, his eyes twinkled the way they used to. It was as if the sun had broken through deep clouds. She smiled back and was starting to say something else when the barn door behind them squeaked open.

"Whoops." Pete nearly tripped over the dog as he stuttered his way back into the yard. "I was just coming in to check on the horses."

"Then come check on the horses." Bob waved him in, obviously enjoying the way he'd embarrassed his son. "Nobody stopping you."

"Actually, no. It can wait. But how about this sunshine, huh?" He looked around, did a quick *Sound of Music* spin, and raised his hands before slamming the door shut once more. "Almost like somebody's been praying."

Bob never let go of Charlotte.

"What do you suppose got into him?"

"You know exactly what got into him, Robert Stevenson. Did you see how red his face got?"

They both had to laugh at that, and Charlotte had no words for how good it felt, after all these weeks. When Bob looked at her again, though, his expression turned a little more serious.

"Were you praying, Char?"

"Maybe not for the sunshine." She pulled away, but her hands still nestled in his. "But for other things, yes. For you."

Chapter
Twenty-Eight

B y the time Charlotte and Bob emerged from the barn a few minutes later, both of them had to stop in wonder at what was going on.

"What in the world?" Charlotte looked all around the yard, from behind the house and all around the barn. "This is looking more like the Adams County Fair than our little open house," said Charlotte.

"That's what I was going to say." Her husband agreed.

Bob's newly constructed food booth had a lot to do with it, but so did the picket-fence pen Sam and his new friend Arielle were erecting. Christopher busied himself setting up a weather-forecasting table, complete with the rain gauge he and Bob had worked on, while Emily and Ashley grunted as they helped wrestle hay bales into place around the perimeter.

Meanwhile several men finished putting up a raised ply-wood platform, while several kids set up the sound system, complete with microphone and twin loudspeakers on tall stands. At the sound guy's signal, a western tune started blaring.

And then the food people! Smoke soon began pouring from the lineup of grills, wafting the wonderful smell of bar-

becue around the farm. A bevy of church ladies set out plat-
ters of salads and desserts, chips and buns, bottles of ketchup
and mustard and bowls of relish. Hannah waved when she
caught sight of Charlotte, and Charlotte waved back.

Another group of kids wearing matching blue-and-green
FFA T-shirts wrestled ten-gallon stainless-steel urns of coffee and punch and who knew what else out of the beds of
two pickups. They parked the urns in a line on a folding
table next to the food booth and ran an extension cord out
to plug in the coffee.

Several girls seemed to have taken charge of the decorat-
ing scheme, setting out poles with streamers and blowing
up balloons with a helium tank. Hand-lettered signs on
poles bore messages like LINE FORMS HERE or PLEASE
WASH YOUR HANDS AFTER VISITING THE PETTING ZOO.

And there in the middle of it all, Pete ran about like a
whirlwind in a late summer cornfield, giving directions,
lending a hand where needed, and pointing out what the
workers should be doing. He seemed to know where each
person should go and didn't hesitate a moment as he
directed this farm ballet of more than fifty volunteers.

Bob just stood watching, his hands on his hips, shaking
his head slowly.

"Never seen such a thing," he told Charlotte. "I had no
idea he had it in him."

"Don't you dare say that to anyone else," Charlotte
warned him. But he held up his hands in surrender.

"I was just saying . . ." He shifted the bill of his John
Deere cap back a notch. "It's impressive, is all, especially on
this short of a notice. He just took the bull by the horns."

"That he did." She slipped an arm around his waist. "Makes you proud of your son after all?"

This time Bob nodded, smiling as he did.

"Guess you could say that."

And then the caravan of yellow buses arrived, bumping down the driveway, each filled with young school kids. As the lead bus honked to announce its arrival, Pete looked with alarm at his watch, then around at his volunteers.

"All right, they're here!" he shouted. "They're early, but they're here. Tour guides, meet me on the platform! Traffic directors, show them where to park! Parking-lot hosts, you know what to do!"

If things had appeared busy before, now everyone sprang into overdrive—including Toby, who barked her eager greetings at the visitors. A crew of six or seven FFA boys in matching hats and T-shirts trotted out to the end of the driveway, each waving a red flag to direct traffic away from the softer, muddier areas and toward the firmer gravel parking areas between the barn, the house, and the tractor shed. The first bus made it through safely and parked in front of the barn. The second bus was not as fortunate, straying off the road just enough to sink its rear wheels into a soft puddle.

"Oh no." Charlotte knew there was nothing she could do to help, but Bob sprang into action, scurrying for his tractor.

Meanwhile, Dana led her charges off the bus, chattering excitedly. Pete trotted up to greet them.

"Sorry about that!" he told her, but no one seemed to mind. Within a couple of minutes Bob had brought up the tractor, and Pete had secured a tow rope under the front of the bus. Never mind the mud.

"Ooo," said one of the fourth graders who stood around to watch the rescue operation. "He's getting all muddy."

Pete crawled out from under the bus and signaled to his dad to take up the slack.

"That's what farmers do," he told them in full tour-guide mode. "We get dirty. In fact, this is my specialty."

Fortunately it didn't take much to pull the bus back onto the firmer part of the gravel lane, and soon they had all three buses safely lined up in front of the barn. From there, teachers and parent volunteers corralled their students in a semicircle around the main platform, and Pete's voice boomed over the sound system.

"Welcome to Heather Creek Farm," he told them. "And on behalf of the Stevenson family, we're glad you're here. This place has been in our family for five generations . . . going on six."

He paused to look at Sam and Emily, who stood off to the side, while the young crowd applauded.

"So let me bring up that sixth generation right now, and then we'll get you assigned to a tour. Sam? Sam's the red tour leader, along with his able assistant Arielle, for everyone who has a red card. Let me see those red cards right now."

About thirty kids held up their cards and cheered until Pete raised his hand once more.

"All right, good. Now, I'm not going to make you raise your cards again, but Uncle Bill is blue. Emily and Christopher are yellow. Dana and I are green. And finally, Grandpa—that's Mr. Stevenson to you—is leading the purple group, which is going to start over by the barn doors. Okay, teachers? Let's divide up into your groups!"

That's when the crowd started buzzing as people separated toward the five assigned tour guides. Charlotte looked over at Bob, who had fished out a purple cardboard paddle and was waving it up in the air.

"Color coded?" Charlotte couldn't believe it. "Pete has everyone color coded?"

"Dana's idea." Bob called back at her over the rising crowd noise. Some thirty or forty excited kids had gathered around her husband. She smiled and blew him a kiss as she backed away and let him take control.

"All right, now, let's have it quiet!" said Bob, still waving his purple paddle. "We're going to have a chance to see everything you want to see, but first let me tell you the ground rules . . ."

"I am so impressed." Hannah stepped up alongside her, and they walked slowly together back to the food booth. "You have this organized to a T."

"Me?" Charlotte laughed. "My dear Hannah, I had nothing to do with this. It's all Pete and the kids . . . and Bob. I've been laid up for the past several days, as you know."

"Is she trying to be modest?" asked one of the gals behind the serving counter, overhearing the conversation. "We know how organized Charlotte is."

"Girl Scout's honor." Charlotte raised her hand. "This is none of my doing. You got a call from Pete, didn't you?"

"I did," answered the woman—Bev or Beth from First Baptist, Charlotte couldn't remember what her name was. "But he told us he was calling on your behalf."

"That's stretching it." Charlotte still couldn't believe her son had put all this together. But right now, she thought she'd better find a seat.

"Here." Hannah found her a chair. "You don't want to overdo it."

Which was nice of her to say, even if it made Charlotte feel twenty years older. From their vantage point they watched the five color-coded groups crisscrossing the property from the barns to the fields, around the shed, and back to the house.

"Goodness, is there really that much to see?" Charlotte wondered out loud while the barbershop quartet launched into a spirited rendition of "Yes Sir, That's My Baby" and cars and trucks came in a steady procession up the driveway. The parking boys were ready for them, whistling and waving like rodeo clowns as they parked the visitors in row after row and danced between the advancing vehicles.

"The main barn was completed in 1891 by my great-great-grandfather, Albert Stevenson," Bill told his tour group as they came within Charlotte's earshot. He sounded as if he could have done this sort of thing for a living. "He'd brought the family out from Boston, moving them west across the plains and looking for a better life. The story goes that he prayed for guidance, wondering where to go. And when they camped out on the banks of Heather Creek, here, they had their answer."

Ironically, Bill pointed in the direction of the creek that had flooded so many of their neighbors as he went on.

"Great-Great-Grandfather Albert was one of the leading farmers in Nebraska at the time and was even nominated once for state representative. He declined the honor, though, saying he had too much plowing to do. Sort of reminds me of his great-grandson. Now follow me, and as soon as that slowpoke purple group is done, I'll take you into the main barn to show you some of its architectural features. While we're waiting, though, does anyone know where Nebraska's largest barn is located?"

That would be the Starke round barn, near Red Cloud— a fact Charlotte had learned in grade school as well. Even if she couldn't follow around the groups right now, she enjoyed listening to everything going on, from the church ladies cooking lunch to the grandkids leading their own tour groups of school kids around the property. Who would have thought? Families and grandparents and neighbors and . . .

"You come back here!" Christopher hollered as he came flying around the corner of the barn, right on the heels of a white-faced calf. He lunged but came up short, landing face-first on the grass. Meanwhile, the escape-artist calf trotted away through the growing crowds, making a little satisfied grunt and looking back at Christopher as if to egg him on.

"I'm going to get you," cried Christopher, pointing his finger, "if it's the last thing I do."

He promptly stood back up, dusted himself off, and recruited several schoolmates to take up the chase with him. The folks around the lunch booth seemed to think it was great entertainment, and laughed at the kids' progress.

An hour later, Christopher's calf had been safely corralled once more, and Toby had settled down enough so they didn't need to tie her up on the porch, the way Charlotte had feared. Meanwhile the side yard and much of the field had filled with cars and trucks, and the school kids had finally finished their tours. Several hundred visitors gathered as Pete took the platform once again and plinked on his microphone for attention.

"Okay, everyone." The crowd hushed as he raised his hand. "We have a special presentation to make before the lunch line officially opens, and for that I'd like to call up the central Nebraska regional director of the Farm Family Foundation, Mrs. Julie Gauge."

Now everyone applauded as a forty-something woman in a dark navy skirt and blouse stepped to the microphone. She looked more like a politician than a farm girl, smiling broadly as she took the microphone.

"I want to thank the Stevensons for the wonderful hospitality today, and especially . . ."

She had to pause for the applause to die down.

"And especially for Charlotte and Bob Stevenson, who operate this farm and who have worked so hard to give their grandchildren a wonderful place to live and grow up. This is the spirit of Nebraska at its best, where honesty and hard work are at the core of our family values from generation to generation. Come on up here, you two, and bring the whole family, would you?"

Again she had to pause as everyone clapped, including and especially Arielle in the front row. Charlotte felt her own cheeks warm as Bob helped her from one side and Pete helped from the other. Who said anything about getting in front of all these people? Charlotte motioned for the three kids to follow, and Bill brought up the rear with Anna. Jennifer and Madison must have been hiding, but that was okay. Still the crowd cheered.

"Is there any doubt why the Stevenson family was chosen Adams County's Nebraska Farm Family of the Year?" Julie Gauge asked the crowd, which cheered all the louder.

What have we done to deserve all this? wondered Charlotte as Julie Gauge proceeded to give them their gift certificates and more accolades than seemed fitting. She knew the answer was "absolutely nothing" but couldn't help thinking how perfectly the event had turned out—despite the fact that she herself had done almost nothing to arrange it.

Maybe the most perfect things are the ones I have no control over, she thought. And in her own life, she thought perhaps that was true.

At the same time, Charlotte looked out at the smiling faces of people she loved, and she couldn't keep the tears from flowing.

There was Eulalia Barry, holding her precious little cat, Risky, in her arms. And Dave and DeeDee Meyers, whose farm had been submerged but who had still done so much to help everyone else around them. And of course Hannah and Frank, who stood arm-in-arm at the edge of the crowd. What would Charlotte do without neighbors like them?

Mercifully, Julie Gauge's presentation finally wound to a close, and she surrendered the microphone to Pete. He gave a few instructions and reminded the crowd of the farm demonstrations being put on by the FFA kids throughout the afternoon.

"And, oh yeah, the food!" He acted as if he had forgotten, and naturally that drew a laugh from the crowd. So he explained how the lines would operate and who was to thank for all the hard work. Yet again the crowd joined in applause.

"So we're going to have Pastor Evans come up here," said Pete, "and he's going to say grace before we—"

"Uh, actually, Uncle Pete." Emily stepped forward, to everyone's surprise. "There's one more thing we need to do before lunch."

Pete obviously wasn't expecting the interruption, and he looked around with a puzzled expression as Emily motioned to her brothers to join her around the microphone. Charlotte knew something was up, seeing little Christopher jumping up and down as if he couldn't contain the surprise. Bob leaned over and whispered in her ear.

"You have any idea what's going on?" he asked.

She shook her head no.

"We, uh, we just wanted to say . . ." Emily hesitated, as if searching for words. Sam apparently caught sight of Arielle in the front row of the crowd; she was beaming and seemed to only have eyes for him.

I'm really going to have to find out what's going on between those two, thought Charlotte as Sam came to his sister's rescue.

"We just wanted to say that our grandparents deserve this, and we wanted them to have something from us."

As if on cue, Bill reached down behind the platform, coming up with a large gift-wrapped . . . What was it? The wrapping paper looked to be a strange combination of Christmas Santas, happy anniversary, and baby shower prints. By the way he wrestled it onto the stage, it was apparently quite heavy and as large as a desktop.

"We made it ourselves!" added Christopher, who helped pull up the gift. "Except that Arielle helped with the lettering. Open it, Grandma!"

Charlotte and Bob pulled at the wrapping paper together to reveal a wonderful masterpiece of a sign, carefully hand-lettered in dark green over a background of white, with a cow head on one side and a horse head on the other. It even carried the official Farm Family Foundation logo in the corner, as Julie Gauge had once promised. But in between, in large letters . . .

"The Stevensons," read Charlotte as Bill propped up the sign and Sam held the microphone in front of her face. "Heather Creek Farm. Adams County Farm Family of the . . ."

Her voice cracked when she noticed the carefully printed names across the bottom: "Bob, Charlotte, Pete, Sam, Emily, and Christopher."

"Oh, kids!"

She couldn't help it. Even in front of hundreds, she pulled all three of her grandchildren into a wonderful group hug. And when she looked to the side, she saw her husband wiping away tears as well. Obviously he couldn't help admiring the sign either—no matter what his earlier objections had been.

"We just wanted you to know, Grandma." Emily told her as the crowd applauded yet again. "We're all in this—"

"Together!" Christopher finished the sentence as Pete resumed his master of ceremonies role.

"Well, I don't know about anybody else," he said, "but I'm starving. Pastor Evans?"

This time Nathan Evans took the microphone, adjusting his wire-rimmed glasses as he addressed the crowd.

"Shall we pray?" he intoned, and the crowd hushed. He began by thanking the Lord for the beautiful weather and for the love of the neighbors here, even through the toughest of times.

"And we thank you for blessing this family, Lord," he added, "Bob and Charlotte, their kids and grandkids—even their animals. For making them a beacon to people around them, examples of those with a servant's heart."

Charlotte found and squeezed her husband's hand, knowing exactly who the pastor meant when he mentioned servants. Bob squeezed her hand back, the way he always used to do when they held hands more often.

She couldn't help peeking out over the bowed heads of the crowd as the pastor's words of thanks echoed out over the freshly plowed fields, where—could it be?—Charlotte thought she saw a pair of gulls settling down on the freshly turned soil, perhaps in search of lunch.

I don't deserve any of this, Lord. She added her own prayer to the pastor's. *But I'm grateful still.*

Grateful for the husband with the rough hands and the soft heart, who didn't always know what was going on but who was willing to give up everything for his family.

Grateful for the sons who always came to her rescue and who she could trust with her future.

Grateful for the grandchildren who were finding a home here—in their own way and in their own time, to be sure, but finding one nonetheless.

And grateful for the friends who prayed for her as they

dropped everything to come and help, even the friends who had experienced so much trouble of their own. What more could she ask for?

The gulls' soft cry blended with the amens of the people. Listening, Charlotte couldn't help recalling the lines of the Frost poem she'd been trying to read during the rainstorm just before the flood, though that now seemed so long ago. How did the verses go again?

> As the uncertain harvest; keep us here
> All simply in the springing of the year.

Amen. The pastor's voice faded as everyone looked up again.

Christopher headed straight for the front of the barbecued beef line. "Amen," he said, loud enough for the microphone to pick up his voice as he walked by. "Dig in!"

About the Author

Robert Elmer is a former pastor and small-town newspaper editor who began writing novels during evenings and weekends, often after the rest of the family was asleep. Today he has written more than fifty books for youths and adults, including *The Duet*, *The Celebrity*, *The Recital*, and *Like Always*. He enjoys speaking at schools, serves on the editorial board of the Jerry B. Jenkins Christian Writers Guild, and lives with his wife, Ronda, near a beautiful lake in rural Idaho. Find out more at www.RobertElmerBooks.com.

A Note from the Editors

This original book was created by the Books and Inspirational Media Division of Guideposts, the world's leading inspirational publisher. Founded in 1945 by Dr. Norman Vincent Peale and Ruth Stafford Peale, Guideposts helps people from all walks of life achieve their maximum personal and spiritual potential. Guideposts is committed to communicating positive, faith-filled principles for people everywhere to use in successful daily living.

Our publications include award-winning magazines such as *Guideposts* and *Angels on Earth*, best-selling books, and outreach services that demonstrate what can happen when faith and positive thinking are applied in day-to-day life.

For more information, visit us at www.guideposts.com, call (800) 431-2344 or write Guideposts, PO Box 5815, Harlan, Iowa 51593.